MISS AMERICA

STORIES BY
DON SKILES

MARION BOYARS
BOSTON . LONDON

First published in 1982 in the United States and Great Britain by
MARION BOYARS INC.
99 Main Street, Salem, New Hampshire 03079.
and by MARION BOYARS LTD.
18 Brewer Street, London W1R 4AS.

Australian and New Zealand distribution by
Thomas C. Lothian Pty.
4-12 Tattersalls Lane, Melbourne, Victoria 3000.

Library of Congress Cataloging in Publication Data

Skiles, Don, 1939
    Miss America.
    Contents: Miss America — The man who taught nude bicycling — The
book jacket — (etc.)
    I. Title.
PS3569.K45M5   813'.54   81-69652
ISBN 0-7145-2755-6   AACR2

British Library Cataloguing in Publication Data
Skiles, Don
Miss America and other stories.
I. Title
813'.54 [F]   PS3569.K/
ISBN 0-7145-2755-6

'The Man Who Taught Nude Bicycling' first appeared in *Floating Island* (III), 1980, Pt. Reyes, CA.

'The Man Who Had Never Been in Tacoma' first appeared in *Sun and Moon,* Numbers 7 & 8 (Special Issue), 1978, Baltimore, MD.

Poems and articles by Don Skiles have appeared in:
The New York Quarterly, Chelsea, Epoch, Tunnel Road (anthology), *En Passant, Loon, La Bas, Grande Ronde Review, Poet Lore, Sun and Moon, San Francisco Bay Guardian, Lycoming Review, Matter, Titmouse Review, Windless Orchard, West Branch, Phantasm, Primer, International Film Buff, The American Book Review,* and *The Bookseller*

To Marian Schell,
who didn't type the manuscript

CONTENTS

MISS AMERICA

Harris woke up in the morning slowly. He had a strange dream, on the borderline of sleep and waking, in which he thought he was in Los Angeles. There he watched with fascinated amazement while a group of film people went through theatricals. A private gathering. Even more amazing, a producer, a natty man with a heavy tan, black pencil-line moustache, and greased hair that struck Harris as somehow ominous even in the dream, asked him to write a film script for him. This was a realization of a dream, thought Harris, but then he proceeded to awaken; the voices of the gay crew at the pastel house in a Los Angeles as clean as it was in the thirties faded, and he became aware of a slight, repeated tapping sound. It was the windowblind on one of the windows, flapping slightly in the early morning breeze. A not unpleasant sound, Harris decided.

The voice he heard then was wispy and high-pitched, and he thought that he must still be in his dream. It came from the other bed in the room, unused since Harris's girl friend — or that's what they used to call them, he said often to himself — had moved out one night while he was working late, leaving him an extravagant dinner in the oven, and a long letter in which she had detailed exactly why she was terminating what she referred to as their 'relationship', a term Harris had an instant and intense distaste for the first time she had said it to him. He had often muttered it under his breath, when he was angry with her, or when driving his car, when he would find himself saying it for no apparent reason, staring out the windshield at the unfolding freeway.

'Relationship, relationship . . . well, it's a *relationship*, isn't it? Paul, you *know* how I feel! You never tell me how *you* feel, I don't know how you feel. . . .'

This was how Julia would go on. Once she had hidden a tape recorder under the coffee table and taped their entire conversation, which was a particularly heated argument that had occurred, again, because of his having to work late. Julia had an inherited income, and although she worked, she really did not have to. But Harris was never sure if this was the real bone of contention between them, so to speak. Julia had been going to a CR group for a number of months; in fact, the tape recording, which she had played back in her room while refusing him entrance, for nearly half the night, had apparently been suggested to her by someone in that group. But that had been before, actually; a fairly good time before, hadn't it? He was foggy with sleep still, and the voice spoke again.

'I like my eggs over easy. With my coffee, please — a touch of lemon is the way I prefer it. Slice the ham very thinly. You *do* have ham, don't you? . . . I mean, what would eggs be without ham?'

There was a light sigh, a swish of bedclothing. Frothiness.

'Or do you have any prosciutto? Oh, with fresh melon! That would be lovely. And fitting, too, I must say.'

So it was. Harris awoke fully, and found that the young woman in his bedroom, in the other bed, was awake and talking about her breakfast, looking at him with wide, but calculating eyes. She was Miss America, of course, as she had told him, and was shocked that he did not realize what had happened. She refused details, and sulked for her breakfast. Harris dutifully went to his small kitchen, frowning. He had returned abruptly then to the bedroom, where the woman was sitting primly up with her back propped on her pillow, reading a *Vogue* magazine. He faced her squarely.

'Miss America is a fable,' he said, looking at her closely.

She raised her eyes and surveyed him cooly, and then went back to her magazine, flicking a page over with a flash of manicured hand that shone in the dull light of the bedroom like ivory and made Harris stir in spite of himself. He cleared his throat, and moved his leg slightly.

'A thing on television. Atlantic City. Advertising rites.'

'HummmmmHpmph!' said Miss America, and her eyes blazed quickly at him. 'A lot you know about it, big fella. Now get my breakfast.'

He was tempted to give out with the customary profane, obscene retort, the healthy four-letter word, followed by a three-letter word, with proper inflection, but he didn't. He needed a little mystery in his life anyway, he thought. The city was boring in its extravagances, and maybe this would rouse him from his lethargy that had gripped him spasmodically, or even torpidly — a wonderful redundancy, that, he thought — since Julia had left.

Julia had gone down to Los Angeles, and then she had sent him a post card from Albuquerque, New Mexico, and then another card from Paris. She had always wanted to go to Paris, he mused. Julia had gotten some sort of job with a computer consultant firm there, and wrote him a letter in which she described McDonald's in Paris, and the awful chic of the Parisian women. The men were super macho, she wrote, with two exclamation points. 'You would not *believe!!*' she followed that with. He did not know if she meant the macho Frenchmen, or some other belief that he had been lacking in.

He rummaged in the refrigerator, and found that he did have ham. He had forgotten that he had it — or maybe he had gotten it when he made his awful Friday night trip to the Safeway, a trip that made him shudder there in the kitchen as if he had suddenly been standing on cold steel.

'The misery of it,' he muttered under his breath to himself as he ground coffee in the electric mill. 'The utter horror of it . . . affluence, and barren acres of foodstuffs. Friday night. Alone, after the Safeway. . . '

That was probably where he had gotten this cute little ham, that the label said was a Hostess Ham, and weighed in, again according to the accommodatingly fixed label, at 4 lbs 8 ounces. Fully Cooked! Ready To Serve! Dee-licious!! That was on the label, too. He decided he would cook the ham, anyway. He would slice the ham very thinly, eh? As she had said.

He felt still halfway numb, there in the kitchen, which looked out through dirty windows across a forest of charming pastel-colored ventilation pipes. Everything in California was pastel-colored, he thought, as he waited for the water to boil. Even the sky was a pastel blue. Once, he had met a girl who had had eyes exactly that color. She had sat down across from him in a snack bar, so called, on the base where he had served in the Air Force. He had lifted up his head from his book, and she was looking right at him, with some terrific purpose in those pastel, china blue eyes. He had gulped, probably audibly, he reflected, thinking back on it. For this young girl was the daughter of one of the mighty commanders of the base; many of the troops groaned over her in their dreams at night, tossing on their beds in the old Nisson hut barracks. The main stud of his squadron had tried to garner her favors, but failed — and he had admitted failure, which meant something extra special, indeed. The girl had spoken to him, and told him, among other things, that she came from California. You could see all the way into her eyes when she talked to you; it was unnerving. He could remember the absolute clarity of them yet, and the equal sensation of hardness they gave out, a brilliant hardness. They were cats' eyes.

He put more coffee beans in the little Moulinex electric mill. It was a cheery appliance, colored orange and white; it always made him think of Europe. It had that designed, neat, yet esthetically considered look that he associated with things European. It was true, he reflected, grinding the French Roast (Dark) beans, that they knew how to do things over there; that they knew how to live. Why was it that this was so vehemently denied in America? Both the knowledge of how to live, to enjoy living, and the knowledge that the Europeans, who were supposed to be old, decadent, tired out, burned up, through, finished, and over the hill etc., knew how to do it; constantly his friends would smile knowingly, and deny this. 'Yes,' they would say, 'but here in America is where it's *really* happening. This is where it is going on baby.' One friend even confided that the Tibetan Buddhists had announced that America was the place of the future; they were therefore establishing themselves in the USA. But, thought Harris frequently, *what* was it that was happening? Everyone else seemed to know; yet he wondered if they really did.

He poured the steaming water over the fresh grounds, and inhaled the aroma he never got tired of. Better than the actual coffee, it was, like the smell of many cigars and pipes. The smell of a cigar on a frosty morning! Harris remembered his home in the East. The Fall. Autumn. Sweaters, and leaves burning, and football games, and car heaters, and gropings under heavy clothing. Girls wore penny loafers and white socks. The shock he had experienced the first time he had caressed a girl with nylons on, after all those bare high school girl legs, still sweetly naive. But the nyloned legs; a different world. . .

'Don't you get any morning paper?'

She had come out, and was standing framed in the doorway of the little kitchen. She had on a velvet sort of robe, which was a shining white color that slightly hurt his eyes. He blinked at her, probably looking truly owlish, he thought.

'You're cute,' she said, and smiled at him, her teeth also a dazzling white light; one felt a rush up one's spine when she smiled like that.

She walked over and picked up the coffee jar, with the fresh ground coffee in it, and smelled it.

'What is this — Italian?'

'French Roast. Dark.' he said, feeling that it was somehow not right. Something was not right, definitely.

She wrinkled her nose, and even that was attractive. He wondered if she could possibly ever look unattractive. But it was not even a matter of attractive; she was beyond that. She did not *look*; she *was*, he thought. Total.

'Jesus, French Roast! . . . Dark!' She laughed, in her throat. Just like the movies. And threw her hair around, and played with the belt of her robe. The cleft of her breasts gleamed. Harris gulped, and pushed his glasses up on his nose, a characteristic gesture with him. Once he had tried to count how many times in a day he did it, but he had gotten hopelessly behind by noon of the day.

'It's good coffee. I get it from a small shop, a local place. Up the street.'

'You've gone there for years!' she cut in. 'Years and years and years and years! Right?'

'No, actually he's only been there for about two years. Or so.' Haris had answered automatically. After the last word, he saw her looking intently at him, her head slightly lowered. She was playing with a curl of her hair, which was a color he had never seen in real life before. Her hair was an auburn red color, very deep, and it shone, even in the dim light of the little kitchen of his small apartment. Everything about her shone, Harris realized. She really was glamorous. It was a fact.

'What's wrong with French Roast?' he said, hurriedly, looking closely at how thinly he was slicing the ham. Then he would not have to look at her. He felt that he could not think right when he was looking at her. He could see her switching the tassels of the belt back and forth, a white movement. He could see her foot come out of the bottom of the full-length robe. His head swam, and he pressed the knife into the cutting board. She laughed.

'You ought to get a coffee that really has something. You ought to get Blue Mountain Coffee. You know; the stuff from that place in Jamaica? Do you know about it?'

She asked rather kindly; it wasn't heavy with sarcasm. Her toenails were painted some translucent flesh shade; her feet were actually tanned, but not heavily. A perfect skin match for her hair. He wondered suddenly if her whole body was tanned; his eyes unfocused, and he gulped again, probably audibly, for she looked quickly at him.

'It's something like twelve dollars a pound,' he said, taking the ham over to the tiny stove.

'That's right. Expensive. It's worth it. Have you ever had it?'

She looked at the ham, and smiled.

'Just nicely cut. Thank you. Now don't fry it very much. Just a tinch.'

'A tinch?'

'A tinch.'

He shook his head slightly, and put the ham in the little frying pan. She was standing very close to him, and the stove. He noticed that he was perspiring.

'You better move back a little; this stove's not too reliable. You know how these places are; the stuff in them. You have to fiddle with everything, you know. The stove here; I had to nearly blow myself up with it. Call the gas company. The landlord sent over some old repairman; some alcoholic fellow, probably a relative. He stuck his head in the oven. With a match! I couldn't believe it. And the refrigerator, the icebox, it had a defective thermostat, and the first full day I had it on, I came home, and opened it, and there was a solid block of ice forming around the freezer part, there. You know those little freezer units, like they have in these old frigs? A block of ice. What was happening, was that the thermostat was overheating, see, and so it was making this tremendous amount of ice. If I had been gone — say, over a week-end — it might have filled the whole top of the thing. This gigantic block of ice! I would have opened the door, and there would have been this gigantic piece of ice, with the freezer unit right in the middle of it. I don't know what I would have done.'

She was watching him as he talked, and he felt like he couldn't stop, so he stopped abruptly, and did not look at her. He turned his back to her, and put the top on the Melitta coffee pot and carried it into the front room, where he sat it on the table. Then he stopped, for he realized he did not know where she was going to eat. He felt suddenly tired, and under a great deal of strain. What was she doing in the apartment, anyway?

'Do you think I could eat my breakfast in bed? After all, I am a princess. I am royal. Don't you think?'

Her voice was very quiet this time, and so soft that he did

have to strain a bit to hear her. He nodded; she walked out of the room and back into the bedroom. It was a relief; he rushed back into the kitchen, turned on the water tap loudly, and took a large breath, then another, that he had been dying to do, almost literally. His heart pounded, and he squeezed his hands, to get a grip on himself; it always worked for him. He closed his eyes for about twenty seconds, then started to fry up the little slices of ham. He would get the rest of it together. Get it all together, as the phrase had it these days. Think as he cooked; it had always been a good time for him to do that, like the times of riding on a train, or in a bus.

He would make, also, some English Breakfast tea, for himself. It always made him feel good, that tea. Irish Breakfast was even better. They had some now that came in beautiful canisters, with the misty colors of Ireland reproduced in photographs on the canister. It made him long to return there, to get back to that country that he had enjoyed so much on a two-week holiday . . . that was a long time ago, though. Everything seemed to be getting to be a long time ago in his life. The present was a blur in which he found it hard to decide what he was doing, or had done, or intended to do. Was this the onset of middle age? And then there was all this business with this Miss America person, in the next room, which was totally uncalled for. He did not need it. Maybe he would have muffins. He could not find them in the refrigerator . . . here they were. Why couldn't he move faster? Be more decisive? She had said something about having been Miss South Dakota before . . . Jesus! Really! Miss South Dakota! What kind of a world were we living in?

The tea smelled good, and the hot water steamed into the brown teapot. All teapots should be brown, he thought. I don't know why, but it's just a good color . . . I've got to figure out something to do, though. Something to do, after eating. . .

He had no trouble with the eggs; he placed the ham and eggs then on a bright, painted plate. The plate carried a reproduction of a Matisse painting; the gaiety of it cheered him. He snuck a bit of the ham for himself. Maybe cook some for himself, with muffins. Coffee, ham, eggs, muffins; some honey.

'Do you want some honey for your muffins?' he called out. He hoped that his voice did not quaver. Sometimes it broke, which was embarrassing.

'Yes! Lovely!' came a clear voice this time. Her voice had such an amazing ability to change and move up and down registers. He nodded to himself, and put a salt and pepper shaker set on the tray. There it was: thin sliced ham, eggs over easy, muffins and honey, a cup of steaming hot French Roast coffee, a tiny pitcher of Half and Half, some sugar in a little crystal bowl he had brought back from Ireland. He winced; he had no real cream, and she would certainly notice that. He had no melon either, but he had placed a fresh Santa Rosa plum on the tray. A trim brown napkin. No flowers. He had no flowers. No rose, for instance, in a bud vase. Something like that was called for, wasn't it?

He took a deep breath, lifted the tray, and plunged across the floor and into the bedroom. She was propped up with pillows, reading *Vogue*. She looked brightly at the tray, and made her eyes big.

'Where do you want this?' He felt the ultimate awkward person, standing there in front of her. She nodded, indicating her lap, sitting up straighter in the bed. He brought the tray over, and placed it close to her, bending down. A light touch came on his arm; he turned, and she brushed her lips on his cheek. He closed his eyes, then straightened up. She was tearing one of the muffins with her teeth, her eyes looking now up at him. The honey on the muffin was golden, and he realized her skin looked like that in certain lights, in combination with her hair. He closed his eyes again momentarily; he could not stand and watch her eat.

Harris decided that he'd put a record on, and then go and check the mail. This would give him more time to do nothing — to think, if he could get to that point. But why

think he pondered, as he put on a Stan Getz record, a lovely
samba thing with the Brazilian guitarist-singer Joao
Gilberto. The music floated out into the apartment. This
could be Corcovado, he thought, looking out the cracked,
painted framed set of windows that opened out as in a
European apartment. The paint was peeling and bleached
by the sun to a very delicate pastel shade. For some reason
he liked that. What the hell; San Francisco was as good as
Rio de Janeiro, or Buenos Aires. People ate too much meat
down there anyway. You got so that you looked at everyone
as if they were a filet, or a sirloin. Then there were the
dictators. . .

'I *love* that music!' She was out into the little front room,
and dancing about. She took him as she whirled by; he saw
the flash of her legs out of the white robe, and then they
were pivoting together and around the little room. He could
not catch his breath, and he felt stiff. His glasses began to
mist over. Close up, her skin had such a fine grain to it that
Harris could not move his eyes from looking at the
smoothness and texture of it. Her mouth pouted out slightly
at the corners; a swelling. She felt very light against him,
when they would swing around another corner of the room,
but there was a substantiality behind the lightness that
troubled him. Her breasts pushed against him as they
turned. He stopped; he was dizzy.

'Come on! Let's dance some more! What's wrong with
you, anyway?'

She stood with her hands on her hips, arms akimbo, head
slightly forward. For some reason, he found the pose
attractive. He tried to speak, but instead licked his lips.

'I . . .'

'You're an idiot, that's what!' she said, and stalked back
into the bedroom, past him, with a warm, full scent that he
had not noticed before. He blinked, and turned.

'I don't know how to dance this type of dance . . . I was
never any good at it. At dancing.'

The record went into the next piece, increasing in tempo.
He walked over and turned it down soft. He noticed that he

was continually blinking his eyes. He had an image of himself as perpetually blinking, pushing his glasses up on his nose, and apologizing for something. For nearly everything, come to think of it. He could hear her flouncing around in the bed. Then her face appeared again around the bedroom door frame.

'Were you ever good at anything?' She stuck her tongue out, startlingly. He was amazed, and again, delighted, and started to smile.

'I bet you were good in school, weren't you? You were the Number One Student; all A's, isn't that right?'

'As a matter of fact —'

She cut in, waving her hand.

'You brought a little red apple to the teacher. You loved your teacher. She smelled like bread and chalk and something else that you couldn't name. You wanted to kiss her and squeeze her. But what you did was; you got all the answers right in English. In the spelling book. You always had your hand up first.'

'I was never that good at spelling.'

'You dusted the erasers after school!' she said, pouted at him, and was gone back into the bedroom. He could hear her throwing a magazine onto the floor.

It was true that he had dusted the erasers, he thought. He could remember sharply, the white dust rising off them in the cold November late afternoons, wondering if he would get home before dark, wondering how many days it was to Thanksgiving, to Christmas . . . But he had never been able to draw, or cut out things in paper, and his penmanship was also very mediocre. That had given him pain. He had never had any of his drawings, or the oval exercises they did in Penmanship, put on the class bulletin board.

'Did you ever drink good hot chocolate? With marshmallows?' Her voice was softer, quieter. The record was faint now; the equally soft notes of Stan Getz's saxophone. He had seen Stan Getz once, up at the old Jazz Workshop on Broadway. He had always admired him, even envied him. That would be a real life; the life of a great jazz musician. He would know what to do now, in this instance.

'. . . on a cold winter night, just after a long bath, with the wind howling outside, and you know that it is so cold out there! And you bundle up in your robe, and you make hot chocolate, and stand at the window — there's that icy frost forming on the glass, and you touch your finger to it, and melt it. You melt a little hole in it, and your finger gets so cold so quickly. You stand there, and watch the snow blowing around in circles.'

'When I was a child, I used to walk around outside, and *then* do that,' he said. The record was over; he switched the amp off, with a snap of electricity that always made him wonder about the wiring in the building.

'Got any Schumann?' she asked. Again, her face was looking at him from the frame of the door. Her hair, he thought, was really fantastic. It was hanging down in an actual cascade of curls and light. Just at that moment, she shook her head, looking at him.

'Schumann? . . .'

'That's right. Robert Schumann. Something like the Fourth Symphony.'

'Yeah . . .'

She walked out into the room, then to the records filed under the stereo system. She started going through them. He stood and watched her; it was a distinct physical pleasure just to watch her go through those records.

'Beatles . . . Ray Charles!' She turned and looked sharply at him. 'The Master of The Baroque, J.S. Bach. Bach's Orchestral Suites . . . that's beautiful! I like that very much . . . The Rolling Stones; this is not one of their good albums, though . . . Taj Mahal, hmmm . . . Randy Newman!' She looked around again. 'Here . . . Beethoven Symphonies . . . Schumann! You do have it.'

'The Fourth Symphony. Other side has the First.' He heard himself speak, and blinked again. 'A pretty good recording; Deutsche Grammophon. Vienna Philharmonic.'

She stood with the album now cradled in her arms. She

nodded and shook her head again, so the hair moved in that magical, light way. He swallowed, and knitted his brows in a slight frown. He did not know what to do, except remain standing where he was. He felt, again, somewhat lightheaded. He needed to eat, but he had not been able to get back into the kitchen.

'You ought to take me to the symphony here. Not the rock concerts. That would be wrong, you see. You do know that that would be very wrong, don't you?'

'Yes,' he said. His voice squeaked slightly.

'And you ought to take me to the galleries, and maybe the museum once in a while, and to the Cuban restaurant down on 22nd Street.'

'The Cuban restaurant, down on 22nd Street?'

'It's very special. Also, we should hear some good jazz every so often. We can go to the circus when it comes to town, and we should go out to the Cliff House every so often and drink.'

'Nobody ever goes out to the Cliff House anymore. It's all plastic. The tourists. They go there.' It all came out in a rush. He groped behind him, thinking of a chair. But there was none there. She waved the record album lightly in the air. Everything she did was with an effortless sort of movement, he thought.

'That's why we go there,' she said, and frowned suddenly at him for just an instant. 'Idiot!' Then she smiled again, and held the record out to him.

'Put this on, will you?'

'I'm going to check the mail then,' he said, feeling unspeakably foolish as he did so. He took the record from her and walked to the turntable. She moved aside and watched him, standing close. His hands were wet, he noticed; he almost dropped the dust cover down again as he raised it. He could feel her eyes on him; he felt a heaviness suddenly in his whole body. Struggling, he managed to do one thing at a time, an old psychological stratagem he had learned in the military service. Put the record on the turntable. Turn on the switch. Bring over the arm, manually. Let it get tracking. Turn up the volume, and adjust it, as the first strains of Schumann's symphony came into the room. It was a good recording, he thought, hearing it. It was beautiful. He looked over at her; she had closed her eyes. He dropped the record jacket, and bent quickly; picked it up. Standing up, he felt even lighter. She had opened her eyes — probably hearing the jacket fall on the floor, he thought.

'I'll check the mail, then. Just a minute.'

Going down the stairs. A plausible escape for Harris. The stairs were carpeted with old carpet in some places, although at the second landing, new carpet of an outlandish orange and green pattern had been installed. The sudden assault of these colors, after the muddy tones of the old carpeting, was indeed shocking.

There is no elevator in the building, Harris thought as he descended. How many times have I done this? How many times will I do it again? Yet to come? . . . Maybe I will get a new apartment. Down now finally to the first floor, having come through a remarkable assortment of odors on the way; frying fish of an Oriental couple on the third floor who argued every night, the gist of the argument being that the man had other women, while the faithful wife stayed home listening to recordings of Chinese operas, or watching television, both of which she did at full volume. Mrs. Guiterriez, in Number 8, raised in Hong Kong, speaks fluent Chinese, listens to these arguments and tells Harris all. She herself is Portuguese, but speaks mainly English . . . The perpetually stoned-out left-over hippie in Apartment 5, man; the smoke of another pungent day already fulsome around his door. A record playing behind it. All day like that; every day. In Apartment 4 they have been frying potatoes again; rancidness in the heavy air of the hall. Improper ventilation in the entire building. Mice now found all over the place; rampant. The landlord says this entire area of the city is overrun with mice, etc., etc. . . . A thin sliver of pale, milky light from the old glass door out at the front of the hallway; the chilly, damp hallway, always semi-dark, even at midday. Step out into the sounds of rushing traffic. The newspaper rack has the latest edition: Legionnaire's Disease Strikes State.

Harris found two circulars in his mailbox, one from a burial society called The Watchful Eagle Society, and the other urging him to buy a new soap product, along with a letter from Julia with what looked like some sort of Italian stamp on it. 900 lira. Michelangelo print. Green tinted paper; postmark Roma. Open it up; may as well read it now.

A thin sheet of air mail stationery. Date, and time designation: 2.30 am. Rome.

Dear Paul,

Always wanted to visit Rome. Now I am here, and wonder if I really am. Were you ever here? . . . I can't remember if you told me you were, or not. You told me of being so many places over here, and I'd never been here, and that used to make me so damn mad!

What am I going on for, though? It's so early in the morning here in Rome, and you are over there, halfway across the world. I don't even know what time it is over there. I am alone in my room here. And I started thinking, wondering, what you were doing back there in the apartment, and then I decided that I'd just write you a note, at least, and tell you I was here. Sort of a vacation, in a way. Things have been happening at such a clip, you would not believe it, Paul! Everything over here is different, so different; I'm still not used to it . . . I wonder if one ever gets used to it.

Rome is like a big museum, with so much outdoors; the fountains, the buildings, everything. The Romans are shameless thieves, too. The men are worse than in France. Unbelievable. But I like it!

I just wanted to write you something. I will be here for four more days. Caio!

Julia

Rome . . .

Harris went back into the building after sniffing the salt air, with wisps of fog from the night before. The foggy belt of the city, where his apartment was. Back up the stairs and to the apartment, where Miss America was. Unbelievable.

She had gotten dressed while he was downstairs. She had on a pair of French cut jeans, and a shirt that was obviously form-fitted. There was a light green scarf knotted around her throat, and she had a beige sweater and her bag lying on a chair. His stomach rumbled; he still had not had time to eat. He ignored her and walked directly into his kitchen. She was smoking a cigarette by the window, looking out; she did not say anything as he walked by. He cut an English muffin, and put it in the toaster. Maybe he would have some of that ham.

'Hurry up and eat. I want to go out — let's go for a long drive, over across the Bay. It's a good day for that.'

'It's cold out. Probably be foggy later. I have to eat.'

'Poor baby,' she said, shaking her head exaggeratedly. 'Has to eat his breakfast, and start the day out verrrrry slowly.'

She sat down by the window, on the little sofa, and started leafing through another magazine. He could not recall so many magazines being in the apartment. Had she brought them? He hurried with his muffin, and skipped the ham, drinking some lukewarm English Breakfast tea that he had forgotten he'd made. He ate a Santa Rosa plum, and then they were back down the stairs, and out into the car, and he was driving over the Golden Gate Bridge; she was leaning back in the seat, letting her hair flow in the airstream, and the radio was playing some sort of vintage 1930s Dixieland jazz. Muggsy Spanier. The sun came out, and the sailboats were gliding, far below, on the bay. She smiled, and he swallowed again, and looked down on the road; he had to correct his steering a little bit. It was windy on the bridge.

They went to Tomales Bay, to an oyster house, and ate oysters, and watched the sun glinting on the famous bay. He told her that there were more great white sharks in this particular body of water than anywhere else in the United States. She told him about being Miss America. It was all a myth of course, but a very necessary one. She told him about her girlhood. She had had pigtails, and ridden a horse. She had been a cheerleader, and then switched to being a majorette. Better for the poise. She had been seduced by an airline pilot when she was fifteen, and did babysitting for him and his wife. He had taken her home in his customized Thunderbird, a vintage car; he was forty years old.

He told her of his largely uneventful life as they drank a second carafe of wine and watched the sun setting in gold red streaks on the bay. He had worked his way through college as a postal clerk, a messenger, a copy boy on a newspaper, an airlines reservations agent. (She told him that at one brief moment in her life, she'd thought of being a stewardess. Actually thought of it! she said, shaking her wonderful hair, that caught all the sunlight and glowed, honey-colored now.) He had gotten on the Dean's List several times; in his Senior year, he had had a straight A average. He had graduated and got his first job, and then plodded on, to the point where he was now. He worked very hard, always. Was it worth it? she wanted to know, leaning over the table. Was it really worth any effort at all? Didn't he hate it? He did. But he did not know what else to do. The wine was making his eyes feel heavy, and his head loose. He noticed that other people in the little restaurant were staring frequently at their table. Of course — how could they not? He began to speak absurdities, as the dusk filled the room.

'You had a tail at one point . . . a literal tail. In your mother's womb. You journeyed though eons of time, of biological struggle, in six to nine months.'

She did not interrupt him. She was faintly smiling, he thought.

'I think Julia left me because I took off my glasses. Really! . . . Something happens when you take off your glasses. I mean, if you wear them all the time.'

He took off his glasses, and laid them on the table

between them. She became a golden blur across from him. He felt naked. Something did happen when he took off his glasses; he was revealed, another part of his character was revealed. Julia had said that to him several times, and urged him to get contact lenses. Miss America said nothing, but reached across the table and took his hand. He felt suddenly that she was very far off and had saved him from falling. He peered dimly around him.

'Did you ever hear the story about The Princess and The Pea?' she said, squeezing his hand, then letting go.

He shook his head. He was wondering how he would manage to drive back to San Francisco. To the apartment. To the bedroom. What would he do? The water was striking the piers on which the restaurant sat with louder, more insistent force. The wind had come up, and the fog was suddenly blowing in; he could even see it, without his glasses. Maybe they would never leave the restaurant and be there forever, in the fog, eating Helga's, the cook's, delicious fried oysters.

'That story was a fable, illuminating a truth of reality,' she said.

He wondered if he had heard her correctly.

'It was?' he asked. He reached, and put his glasses on again. She was looking out over the water, at the fog coming in; she looked back at him. He felt a flush through his body again when she looked directly at him, and shook her hair slightly, as she nodded.

'Of course. Don't you know exceptionally beautiful girls are very insecure? That they've constantly got to be reassured they are beautiful? Your mother really didn't tell you about girls, did she? Or your father, either.'

'I learned about it in the bushes,' he blurted out, horrified as he heard himself say it. She smiled, and then laughed. It was true. Helen MacFetters — what a name for a child to bear! he thought suddenly. In the third grade. For a nickle, she would go in the heavy bushes on a hillside, near the elementary school, and pull down her panties. For a dime, she would allow you to touch her. For two dimes, she would touch you. Helen MacFetters had also defied the teacher who would not allow her the call of nature; she had straddled the wastebasket near the rear of the room, while the teacher wrote on the blackboard and the astonished children kept quiet, and Helen quickly completed her business. The old maid schoolteacher, Miss Hill, who really was an old maid, was so stunned by the act that she stood speechless and then burst into tears and left the room. Helen MacFetters had been taken out of the class, and she had never returned.

Miss America was finishing her wine. She was still smiling; she rolled the glass around lightly in her hand, holding it up to the window. Now the little candle was lit on their table, in its small red glass, covered with what was supposed to be a piece of fish net. It felt wonderful in the place, Harris thought. Very warm.

'You know, what you ought to do is you ought to do everything backwards in your life,' she was saying. She peered through the wine glass at him, and made a sudden face at him. 'That's what you need. You ought to leave your doors open in your apartment, for instance.'

'Leave my doors open?'

'I mean inside the apartment. You close them every night, right? And then you go around checking everything. Check to see if the lock is chained up right. Check to see if the water's not dripping in the shower. Check to make sure the oven is turned off; check to see if all the lights are really turned off. Check to see if you set your alarm clock, which you set an hour earlier, and already checked a half hour after that.'

It was true. He looked down at the table. There were numerous wet rings from where he had been placing his wine glass. Water was beaded up on the carafe and looked, he suddenly thought, very good in the candlelight.

'You know I'm near-sighted,' he said. It was all he could think of, for some reason.

She was looking again out towards the bay. It was dark now. He could feel the presence of the fog shrouding the restaurant already.

'Well?' she said, lifting her glass to drink.

'One morning I flushed Julia's ear-rings down the toilet, due to it. An accident. We had to get the plumber.'

She winced. Of course, it was all wrong. He wondered why he had said what he had said. It had just come out. What kind of an explanation was that?

'You know how expensive they are. Plumbers make a fortune these days,' he went on. He felt a sudden numbness. She turned swiftly and glared at him, banging her glass on the table.

'Jesus! Plumbers! You talk about plumbers!'

'I know,' he said, hopelessly.

She shook her head back and forth, and leaned forward. Her hair brought that scent again to him, and he closed his eyes for a second, then opened them. She was very close, and looking right into his eyes.

'Everything you say is predictable. You know? It's like — you're like one of those girls that'll tell you how she looked all over the city, in the chic-est shops, of course, and found exactly what she was looking for in Woolworth's! That's wrong, see? It's boring. Boring.' She tapped lightly on the table.

He looked, for some reason, swiftly all around the room, and then gulped, and pushed his glasses up on his nose. He had to say something. She was looking expectantly at him.

'I'm nearly forty three, and I don't know what I'm doing,' he said, again having the feeling that he was blurting out something terrible. She looked momentarily down at the table, but then looked again directly at him. He had to go on.

'I don't have any ideas. I can't think. I don't know anything. I don't know what I want, even. Everybody knows what they want! . . . I don't even know how to drive a car, really. All my friends are buying stocks, real estate. Driving Mercedes. Peugeots. They go to Tahoe on the week-ends. They have positions, you know? They smoke cigars.' He felt drained, and leaned back in his chair. She was smiling suddenly again.

'You're miles ahead, and you don't even know it. Do you?'

'Do I?' He shook his head. 'I don't possess anything. Except debts!'

She laughed, and nodded. It made him feel better.

'I mean, I have only *one* major credit card in my wallet. I don't even have an airlines card. A man my age. That's failure, isn't it?'

She laughed now more fully, out loud, and some people looked around, taking advantage to stare longer than the normal allowed staring time.

'You're great!' she said, and reached over for his hand again. To his amazement, she put it up to the side of her cheek. The touch was so warm that he felt completely dazed, and shut his eyes again quickly, then reopened them. 'Just great. Believe me. Now, let's get out of here, okay? The fog's coming in pretty heavy. We have to get back. Pay the check. Leave a good tip, too. Remember.'

Then it was back over the Golden Gate Bridge. Such a famous bridge; such a famous arc over the waters of the bay. In 1935, there had been no bridge; he had seen photographs showing the skeleton of the famous final work, and read fierce denunciations of the wrecking of one of the greatest natural views any city ever had, published in the newspapers of the time. But now the bridge and its environment were so fused that it was difficult to think of them separately. Driving across it was always a small sort of excitement. With her in the car, he felt it was a time he could never forget. Looking over, she was laying back in the seat, and again the wonderful hair, that looked like it did on those models in magazines, was streaming over the back of the headrest; it was in glorious profusion. For a second he thought of Pope's poem, *The Rape of The Lock.* Then he thought that only he would think of such a thing at such a time. But that was the way he was, wasn't it? And why couldn't he be, why shouldn't he be, the way he was? He suddenly recalled the professor droning on, in a summer-heated classroom, with the laziness and fullness of July, high summer, outside; all that verdure the professor had said, gesturing out the window . . . the poem, with the professor's explanations, had been much more than he thought it was when he first read it. He had felt that he might be the only one in the classroom who even remotely cared about the poem, let alone like it. He had looked at the balding professor in some wonderment, trying to figure out how he could generate the enthusiasm he so obviously had, with the blank looks and ominous quiet in the room. It was known around the college that his wife had died, after a long painful illness that spring. He had hardly missed a session, but his face had changed.

Miss America was talking again; she had been very quiet, letting the fog-filled air stream in the window until his neck was cold, and aching, but he would not tell her of course. Her voice was very soft and so near to him in the car; again he blinked his eyes.

'. . . so I used to write it all down. You know? I kept everything written down. Every reaction I had to everything that I could remember. Somehow I thought that was important.'

'It is important. I do it. I keep a pad by my bed. Julia always went on about it. But she was the one who had me do it, because I was always getting up at night to write things down.'

'You write your dreams down?'

'Especially my dreams. I went to a Jungian analyst for a year. It's very important to me.'

She pointed. 'Look at the city! Coming up out of the fog! Jesus, it's gorgeous isn't it?' She slapped her hands together, and shook her head at him, and laughed; then she reached over and squeezed his thigh. The car swerved; he stretched his neck.

'That's not good to do, on a crowded bridge,' he said. He knew this was wrong, too, but he did not know what to say.

'I ought to feel your leg up while you're driving,' she said, and she moved closer, and put her hand on his leg again. He smiled.

'We might have an accident,' he said, squeaking. He swallowed; she laughed again, and slid back across the seat. She bent down, and pushed in the cigarette lighter. They were getting near the toll gate. He fumbled in his pants for the change. She was lighting her cigarette; he felt ridiculously awkward again. The seatbelt was blocking his hand. She did not seem to notice that he was having a problem. Finally, he got the three quarters, and slid them into his jacket pocket. He felt he had to say something.

'How did you get along . . . through college, and all?'

'Get along?' She blew a jet of smoke out the half-closed window.

'How did you get your income?' It was awful, he thought. Luckily, they were at the booth, and he hurriedly rolled down his window, fishing then quickly for the quarters. One always seemed in a great hurry at these damn toll booths, he thought. The attendant peered intently into the car, and then got down lower, and almost put his head in the window. But Harris rolled it up smartly, the attendant jerked back hastily, and Miss America laughed, and nodded her head approvingly. They moved off into the fog again.

'Oh, somebody always takes care of me,' she was saying, pulling out the little ashtray on the dash. The ash of her cigarette sparked red, and she looked directly at him. 'Someone will always take care of you, when you're beautiful. They always will. Beauty is its own excuse for being. You know?'

'I guess so,' Harris said, in a low voice. It was quiet in the car. He was afraid she could hear him breathing, or his heart beating. They drove back to the apartment like that, without a word, smoke heavy in the car, from the Dunhill cigarettes she smoked. Harris hoped he would not sneeze. He did not.

Before they got out of the car, she touched him on the arm, looking intently at him.

'You understand me? What I said, a bit ago?'

He did not say anything, not knowing what to say. He ran

his hand over the steering wheel, over and over. They were sitting on Lake Street, in San Francisco, in the fog. His chest felt like it was full of her smell. The fog was muffling the sounds, and the fog horns were giving off their strange, melancholy, echoing sounds.

"What I'm telling you is that I'm not a country girl, and I'm not a small town girl. I don't get sick, and I don't shake all over when I cry. I'm a city girl.' She got out of the car then, and he followed. They walked back to the apartment. The street lights were harsh, garish. The city felt mean, even though it was beautiful.

'I used to read Frank O'Hara's poems at lunch time. Did you ever read him, any of his stuff?'

He did not care anymore what the hell he said. He would say what he thought.

She nodded. She looked good even in the bluish streetlights. His chest felt heavy, and he wondered what he would do. He decided he would go on talking about whatever came into his head.

'I was always doing things like that — reading Frank O'Hara. I didn't care. I always read whatever I wanted to. My mother used to tell me to just keep trying . . . you know, that expression "Hang In There!" She used to say . . . she used to say, "Something will happen." She always used to say that. And I would think — you know what I used to think? I used to think, "Yes, you'll go crazy!" '

She smiled at him, and put her arm through his. They were around the corner then, and he had his key out. The hallway was dark.

'The landlord. He never does anything anymore. Slum landlord, from Greece. He goes back there every year, for six weeks or so, and leaves his sons to maintain this building.'

She was not saying anything, and he could not see her very well in the dark. They started up the stairs.

"He needs — I mean, the building needs — a new garbage chute thing. The one now; it's too small. For this size building. So is the barrel. You know? The barrel, that catches all the garbage when you stick it down the chute.'

'The barrel,' she repeated. They were nearly at his door. He fumbled with his keys again. There was a shamrock on the door, stuck there by an Irish friend on the last Saint Patrick's Day; Harris had never removed it.

'All the garbage comes out all over the place, down there.' He was unlocking the door, and they were moving into the dark hallway, and he ran his hand along the wall; pushed the light switch on. 'So what does he do? He doesn't even get —'. He was following her into the little living room and she was already into the bedroom, her scent into his nostrils. '— he doesn't even get any more pick-ups. He does nothing! He just leaves the whole thing, like that, a big mess.'

It was very quiet, and still. He could hear nothing in the bedroom. He pulled down the blinds in the living room, and sat down on the sofa. He felt suddenly tired, very tired. His hands hung down over his knees. The cushions of the sofa were a dirty off-white; he thought vaguely that he would have to get new ones. Or something . . .

When he went into the bedroom, only one light was on. She looked darker, and was sitting up in the bed. He went over to the other bed, and sat down on it. He had no notion of anything, except the light on her hair.

'I think you probably have those little coasters to put drinks on, when people come,' she said, looking over at him. 'Don't you? So there won't be marks on the wood, on the table.'

He stood up and scratched his head; then spread out his hands in a gesture of resignation.

'My sister gave them to me. I can't throw them out. I don't like them, but . . .'

'Did your mother give you a silver dollar when you left home? So you'd never be without money?'

'As a matter of fact, it was my sister. Again. I got on a bus in Pittsburgh —'

She threw up a hand quickly. 'Pittsburgh! Really, Pittsburgh? It really was?'

'It was Pittsburgh, yes, and I got on the Greyhound bus

down there. The bus was the express bus to Chicago, and there I transferred to the bus out here. My sister gave me a 1922 silver dollar at the bus station. So I would never be broke, she said . . . I had seventy-five dollars to my name. I came out here and lived down in the Marina with an old service buddy, and was a messenger boy at Standard Oil Company.'

He was nearer the bed; he had walked back and forth while talking. He thought he probably should make them a drink. What did he have in his cupboard? he thought. She was looking at him again. He had . . . Royal Gate Vodka. Paul Masson Ruby Port wine. Some Hiram Walker Amaretto, that he had bought under the mistaken assumption that it was another brand, much better . . .

He walked out into the living room again; he had muttered something to her about drinks. She had looked very directly at him. That was it, too; directly. He would make vodka tonics. Jesus! Vodka! Everyone drank vodka; there were billboards sixty feet high, when you came off the freeway, with monster bottles gleaming with the cold, malicious glint of vodka. Wodka, the Russians were supposed to say. And caviar. Harris had never had caviar. He got a lemon out of the refrigerator, ice cubes, and the vodka and Schweppes Tonic Water, and mixed up the drinks. Standing there, looking out again over the curious forest of ventilation pipes, he could see Lone Mountain College looking like some sort of monument, illuminated through the swirls of fog that were rising and falling with the wind. For years he had thought it was some sort of hospital, or Army barracks, until he had been taken to a poetry reading there. Of course, he had also, for years, thought the famous San Francisco Art Institute was some sort of Franciscan monastery, as he rode by it on the 30 Stockton bus, to and from work. Maybe he should put something on his FM radio, he thought . . . it was a fine radio, an Emig. He stood in the doorway of the kitchen, looking about the half-lighted rooms of the small apartment he had lived in for — what was it, four, five years now? Julia had found the place.

She had called him excitedly from a small Chinese
restaurant; told him first that they had marvelous won-ton,
and then told him about the apartment. 'In the Richmond!'
she had said. 'Where nobody lives! I've never even lived in
the Richmond! It's where all the Chinese move 'up' to, after
they work in a restaurant in Chinatown for thirty years,
washing dishes, saving all their money to buy a house in the
Richmond.' He had never been able to enjoy eating in a
Chinese restaurant afterwards; he would vaguely, or not so
vaguely, recall the reason why the meals were so
inexpensive.

He had put pictures on the walls to make it better. Julia
had approved. There was a small reproduction of a Roy
Lichtenstein painting, called *Brattata,* on the wall by the
little antique washing stand, with marble top, that Julia had
found on a vacation in Pennsylvania. A real Eastern antique.
There was also an antique ship captain's lamp on the table,
with a mica shade, that probably was worth something. It
cast a wonderful, intimate warm light. A Vargas girl, framed
in a silver and black Art Deco frame, was on the wall
opposite the Lichtenstein. In the kitchen he had a de
Koonig reproduction, *Woman Sitting.* And in the
bedroom . . . two framed Mark Rothkos, and a Clifford
Styll. The Rothkos were all right, but the rest was wrong, he
thought. At least, the walls were all white, an off-white,
too . . .

He took the drink in to her and did not give her one of the
coasters that his sister had given him. She said nothing;
widened her eyes at him, and tilted her glass to him before
drinking.

'Cheers,' he said, weakly.

'All you need now is a Harris tweed jacket, with a paisley
ascot, grey slacks, and a V-neck sweater. Very British.' She
drank again. He could see that she had a peach-colored
nightgown on; perfect for her skin. He wondered where she
had gotten it.

'One time I told this fellow at work that the best tweed
jackets were these famous ones from the Farallon Islands.

Then he went around saying that for quite a while, until somebody else told him.' He had almost finished his drink already. Maybe he would make another.

'That was cute,' she said, and did not smile.

'Okay,' he said, feeling tired suddenly.

'Come over here and sit on the bed,' she said then, patting a place by her. He walked over, and sat down.

'I feel like a kid,' he confessed. Then he drained off the rest of his drink, and held the glass up to the light, squinting at it. 'One time I was actually at the Bombay airport. In India. Can you believe that? Me? . . . It was raining so heavily, I couldn't believe it. There's one place over there — I can't remember the name of it — it rains over four hundred inches a year there.'

'I think it's in Assam,' she said. 'I have a beautiful dress from there.'

'Yeah, that may be it. Want another?'

She shook her head. 'Do you remember when you were a teen-ager?'

'I guess so,' he said, and put his glass on the floor. He tried to remind himself not to trip over it later, or step on it. He should have set it on the table.

'Remember when they had all that stuff about heavy petting?'

'Heavy petting?'

'Yes, and the girl would praise you by saying how much restraint you had; how she admired and respected you. She really respected you. You must remember that.'

He shook his head. He really wanted another drink. She was very close in the bed. It was all crazy, he thought. Totally crazy, the whole business, and happening in his life. Everything that ever happened in his life was totally sane, and crazy, and he could never figure it out, and he never would, but he would perpetually be trying to, and often in advance.

'That was a long time ago,' Harris said, softly. He thought he would cough.

Miss America had her eyes closed. Her eyelashes were, he

thought, the longest and thickest he had ever seen. When she opened her eyes behind them, it was an event. And he felt sure they were real. She drank off the last of her vodka tonic.

'That was shitty vodka in that,' she said, handing him the glass. She started to reach for a cigarette on the end table, but stopped, and looked at him closely.

'You know what this guy said to me once? A guy who was over here from Europe, a big-timer.'

Harris shook his head again. She was almost leaning in front of him.

'He said he loved to fuck American women. "They're always so bouncy, so healthy. So wholesome, and eager to please." That's what he said to me.'

'Would you like to have sex with me?' she asked then, in a sudden quiet tone, really looking up from underneath the heavy, lowered lashes. Her eyes, so clear, glistened. She said it as if she were asking him if he would like to partake of a particularly fine meal at a first class restaurant.

Harris took a deep breath and gulped, or swallowed, but he always seemed to himself, to gulp at these sorts of times. His voice came out nearly strangulated, guttural, thick, and his voice broke on the last word and went up high, like an adolescent's.

'I guess I would.'

'Look at my tits,' she said, putting something into the pronounciation of the word that made his mouth instantly dry. She drew back her gown. He uttered a sighing sort of groan that came out of him even before he knew it. He shook his head in wonderment. She smiled, and covered herself again.

'That's nothing. Look at this.' And she rolled over suddenly, with a hiss of garments.

The buttocks, Harris thought, his eyes hurting strangely. The gluteus maximus, so called. Hers were like carved ivory, and shone. There wasn't a wrinkle there, nothing but a taut, smooth, full swelling, and an incredibly deep cleft. Actually, it looked more like polished marble. Finely grained, polished marble. Harris felt weak. He put out a finger, hesitant. She did not move. He grazed his finger lightly down the marble.

'Jesus. Jesus H Christ.'

She smiled at him, over her shoulder. Again the heavy lashes.

'What an ass,' he said reverently. It was true what they said in all those men's magazines, all those raunchy stories. He knew he would never forget this sight, even if he went no further. Thirty years later, he thought, he would remember and sigh reverently. It was like a cathedral, seen in the full sun suddenly, dazzlingly. He knew, too, that no other woman would be able to make him forget, or want to forget, that marvel. It was really a high work of art. It deserved praise, laudation. Any man would understand, especially if he had seen as Harris had.

'Lord have mercy,' Harris said, not really thinking of what he was saying. He was smitten, with a high emotion, a mystic trance almost. He felt like he was sleepwalking. He drew his finger down over her again, this time from the incredible running sheet of her back. His hand, and his legs, were trembling. He cupped his hand, and squeezed slowly. He thought he was about to swoon.

'That's enough,' she said then, flouncing over again. 'That's plenty. Isn't it?'

'I don't know,' he said, puzzled, feeling like his ears were wrapped in cotton, and burning. She suddenly seemed a long distance away. He did not know what she wanted him to do.

'What was going through that head of yours?' she said, and suddenly rapped his head lightly with her knuckles. 'Eh? What were you thinking about? What were you thinking of?'

'Thinking of?' he repeated in a slight voice.

'That's what I said. You're not deaf.' She had pulled the bedclothes up around her suddenly. 'You hear perfectly well.'

'What was I thinking?'

'Yes. That is what I said. Tell me what you were, or are, or ever did think. Right now!' She pounded her hand on the bed. He sat back, and took a breath. He pushed his glasses up on his nose.

'I was thinking of samurai warriors.' His voice broke, as he hoped it wouldn't when he said it. She closed her eyes briefly, and shook her head, then nodded.

'Samurai warriors. You were thinking of samuarai warriors. Really.'

'Yes . . . they used to hide erotic haiku in their bosoms. In between their iron armor and their silk shirts. About their loved ones.'

There was no sound in the room, and Harris felt like some sort of hush had fallen over everything. He looked down and studied the quilt on the bed; the figured frames of it. He could see the second hand on his watch moving around; it suddenly seemed very vivid to him. Then his glasses were removed very smoothly, and her eyes were up close to his.

'Don't you say another word,' she said. Her arms were so warm around him that he knew it must be a dream; her eyes were so close he couldn't look anymore and closed his own. He wanted to say something about what a big effect glasses have on one's whole, entire life; how they can really probably make a central difference in the way you see, and live. But he forgot it.

Later, he was writing a lot of letters, he found. Harris liked to write letters with a Cross pen, that was 12-carat gold-filled, and had a felt tip. A friend of his had received it as Best Salesman of the Year, and had given it to him. In his letters, he wrote about reading Dashiell Hammett's *The Maltese Falcon,* which he was delighted to find took place in San Francisco; he wrote about taking a vacation in London, also. He very much wanted to go back to London, and feel at home. It was probably all a bunch of crap, what the papers and television were saying about England, anyway. He thought he might ride across America on a train — the marvelous romance of trains! In his far-away boyhood, he had lived next to a railroad highgrade and felt the house tremble as the train roared near, and then the windows shaking wildly as it slashed past, just a few feet from the house. He could still remember the old passenger station — Pennslyvania Station — in Pittsburgh, when it was really active. He had sat there full of excitement, wondering where all the people were going. He had seen a silver train on one track; a transcontinental special. He had thought to himself that someday he would take that train. Then he had grown up. He did not write to his friends about Miss America.

Of course, she had to leave. He knew that very early. What was important was that she had appeared, materialized, as it were. He wasn't going to ask any more questions about any of it; it seemed important not to. No more questions.

So he was there, again, in his little apartment, and looking out over the angled roofs and the familiar forest of pastel-colored pipes. Juia had gone to Vienna, and was then going on to Berlin. She wrote about the coffee houses of Vienna, and the wonderful prohibition of cars in the inner city, and the Vienna Opera. Harris got up and put a recording of Brahm's Second Piano Concerto on. The third movement. He sat by the window, which he had opened slightly, and looked out. The window blind made a slight flapping noise; the air had the ocean wetness in it. He looked out over the pastel rooftops and lights and mists. It was very romantic, and he was glad he had a good stereo. It was a Fisher, actually, one of the best.

THE MAN WHO TAUGHT TAUGHT NUDE BICYCLING

Observing the yellow chair in the library. Somebody telling the story of a glass-blower down at an art show. Gave her a hunk of glass; said he was a Swede. She says he was European; or so he seemed, because of a tiredness in his voice. Ages of another experience behind him. And the glass.

To sit there. Come in and hear the rustle of papers, dry coughs, eyes peering furtively. Every day you go there, eh? Piece together *The Complete Guide To International Teaching* on Xerox. At noon, eat some potato chips and a BLT and Coke. Snickers of secretaries, and pompous ties of young lawyers. Old man in the side booth, with rheumy eyes, shovelling soup into a quivering mouth.

You know that somebody has to tell about all this. You know it and shift uneasily. Don't you? Poets drink beer, and watch baseball on television these days, too. Fact. Fact. More fact. And the construction of ink is not as that of milk, or flesh, either. He sees that at dawn through cigar smoke haze and the smell of his sweated socks, the old floor smell. So he lies down there, and we found him, buck naked, rolled up in the rug, later.

Lots in the papers these days about water and fish. As a matter of fact, endocrinology is no doubt the coming science of the coming century. Sitting in a carrel, a naked foot sliding in and out of a sandal says it must be so. The pigmies of the Congo rain forest are being taught how to use baby bottles. Potato chips sleep safely in specially treated bags that admit no light. Freshness.

My friend Harold has been researching the mystique of two swimming pools. Desirable properties now contain two, you know. But he laments. He has gotten side-tracked.

He found a book on the secrets of the Great Pyramid and tells me that language is breaking down. And he is trying to write a poem on the epic roots of the juniper tree he saw in California. He complains, too, of smoking too much and that his hair is already greying at thirty-five.

'How will I now grow old gracefully?' he asks me.

Some people are painting a lot of fish paintings, and evoking thus the very ancient totem of the whale, the Leviathan, the sea-change, the Deluge, Atlantis, the antediluvian world, and the necessary construction of the psychic ship. Long forgotten and neglected, this lore, this study. No key on the chain at night, and so The Wise Old Man does not come. A cold crisp beaded gin is offered at 4 a.m., in chambers. Soft firelight on the walls at Cambridge, where Hurley told the story of Conn-Eda, and St. John Chrysostom. Golden Mouth, kissed the statue of Mary. Everybody waiting.

'Something will happen,' Hurley saying, nodding.

Those are all the fine points of going in and out of the mammoth library. You know what I mean. There is a long gravel path that stretches to the portals, which are huge and stony. Soft heat of the waning day captured in the stones. They found an old beggar sleeping there two nights ago, and turned him away; he urinated on the steps before he left, and some said a strange yellow rabbit peeked out of his coat pocket as he hobbled off. Hurley said it was probably only the reflection of light. A redaction.

'Real Music For Real People' is advertised on the radio now. Twenty-four hours a day.

The science of umbrellas and rain upon them was another topic several people were researching. I remember. We all stood at Land's End, and the lighthouse shone, and when the umbrella was put up, the wind tore it out to sea. What legend in that? That was what I wondered, as we all stood there, looking. My feet were wet and bare and cold, in buffalo-hide sandals bought in a Mexican gift and curio shop in Pittsburgh, and I was trying to get my mind off that. They looked good on my feet, but I could never somehow get the hang of walking in them. I always shuffled along, wearing them.

At least fruit will bloom this year. They say this over the radio, in the early morning reports. Insect control is good. I killed a strange bug, though, late last night; brownish, a white stinger lunged madly from it as I crushed it, as it writhed. I threw it out the window, thinking the sexton beetles would dispose of it properly. Or a bird would, in early light of morning, homing right in on it there. My tea got cold as I sat and thought of all that.

You know how colors come forth from the sound of a train; late at night, the whistle sounding. Don't you?

Later, I could not control it, and I sprayed the room with one of those canned insect repellents. Yard-Gard. Then I had to leave the room, the smell nauseating me with a slight headache, like the sounds of train-cars squealing as they're shunted in a railyard. And I was, sure enough, bare-footed; the white floor was surprisingly cold, and I found my sandals, and discovered that sandals can be warm, if you previously had none.

They say the races this year will be lively, and Riggers is researching the career of Nuvolari, the great Italian driver, who was the prototype of Italian Futurism, and a hero worthy of Mayakovsky, Riggers says. Nuvolari — beautiful name, isn't it? Like the name of a star, or a super-nova, or the incantation of wind, light and speed. Turner should have painted Nuvolari; been alive to paint him. He used to pound his hand wildly on the side of his race car. That was another age.

Ever get a lighted match stuck on your finger tip, as you cup your hand to light a cigarette?

Riggers and Hurley and a small research team meet at a local bar these days. In fact, I'm told they've been meeting there for quite some time. The nature, the exact and precise scope, of their research focus is not clearly known, outside the circle. Some say it is the Tarot. I have heard it is the sounds people make before they die, and one person told me it was a mysterious sort of nocturnal insect which has been known to appear in people's homes at night, buzzing, but never seen. Riggers once laughingly told me it was the hands of 15-year old girls, beautifully eloquent in their formation and luminosity. I can believe that.

I was shown some letters received on another project tangent, before they were cataloged and filed.

'I am sick of trying to be "normal"', one said. 'I am tired of others' expectations.'

'The main thing is that we're not taken seriously', another said.

'Maybe I live in the wrong area, but I see no real change in the attitudes of many people', said a third.

And a fourth said 'Why do people think they have any right to tell me what I should feel inside?'

And still another said 'It's a personal thing, isn't it?'

These are all read through carefully, and computerized for indexing.

Knitting needles click in Lavrinsky's seminar. A horse-fly penetrated there Tuesday a week ago, and has since been mythologized. It finally did escape, when someone opened a window. And they can give you a nasty bite, those things. They say they are attracted especially to heat, and grow lassitudinous, often perching on the cozy inside of a lampshade, near the lighted bulb.

There is talk of new doors being put in at several places here, to facilitate the various research units' inter-communication. One team only recently returned from Rio, where they went to corroborate *Black Orpheus*. How they had changed! They had been outside nearly all the time, and their teeth glinted. One fellow now is to be constantly found in the lavatory, flossing his teeth industriously. He went to a dentist down there, who gave him a red liquid to drink, and then shone a black light in his mouth.

'See that?' the dentist said. 'That yellow stuff, those patches? That's *plaque. Plaque.* You've got to get rid of it.'

They eat a lot of meat down there, too. Lots of beefsteaks, from the Pampas. But that is nothing, if you know what I mean. What I mean is Japan where they feed beer to cows, and professional masseurs work them over daily, to ensure really tender steaks for select restaurants. No gristle in those places. Or joints, as Hurley remarked, laughing.

So with doors and windows at the place now, things progress vigorously, apace. We are indeed pressing on. Azaleas bloom, people are using boats on the river near by, and you can smell the lilacs. So lavender they are! And the other night the professor had a tea, with cheese and biscuits, and we were all nude, you know. I don't know, though, how that actually did transpire, or come about, except that it might have been discussed while we were sailing a while back and heard some birds.

It's being looked into, though. Bet on it. Do.

THE BOOK JACKET

The author said he had served in Intelligence, in the Air Force. Cryptography. He had his picture taken in a very white T-shirt with his nipples showing, glowering into the camera from beneath bushy eye-brows. They'd been made up to look bushy, and he'd sucked in his gut, like a model. He rarely glowered and was a mild-natured, bookish man, who did not smoke a pipe, wore tweed jackets and had never been a professor. He had earned money as a professor, yes.

He had never been a cryptographer in the Air Force, but he did work in Wing Intelligence; even had a Top Secret security clearance. He worried about the spots on his arms.

He had the book jacket picture taken wearing a finely tailored Glen plaid suit, soft blue shirt, and solid color tie, in profile, examining a manuscript. It was not a manuscript, but the photographer wanted him to be looking at something.

An outdoor shot, on a bridge over the Seine in Paris, since it was an international house publishing him. He wore a Burberry trench coat, soft Italian gloves of gazelle, and smoked a cigarette. The belt was looped and tucked just right on the coat. It was shot in a studio set-up in Denver, and they told him he'd get to Paris when the book was brought out there.

His agent thought perhaps he should look serious. One of those serious-looking men who has his photograph taken unsmiling, who you knew would be trouble. Takes himself seriously. An interpreter of history. A beautiful woman will marry him.

He had a white marmalade jar on his desk, in which were pencils, pens, a sword-like letter opener. There was also a white plaster board, off to one side, on which were pinned various items — post cards, three by five index cards with

writing on them, photographs cut out of magazines and
newspapers. An electric typewriter sat on a broad, smooth
table, on which were piles of neatly stacked manuscript. There
was a chair at the table, with a sweater hanging from its back.
Windows cast a luminous, soft, glowing light on the scene.
There were rows of books in a ceiling to floor tier of
bookshelves by the table. The floor was smooth, polished, old
wood with obvious grain. This was his studio.

But it was not the room he wrote in; it was actually the room
of a friend, who was a professional editor. They met in this
room, drank wines his friend collected and discussed stocks,
bonds. He liked wine and owned no stocks.

He was holding a coffee mug in the picture, a heavy Celtic
looking ceramic mug, with a serpent-like coiled handle, and
he had on a cream-colored Aran sweater and corduroy
trousers. He and his wife were standing outside their house
on Long Island or Vermont, or Maine, or Puget Sound, or
Pennsylvania, or Virginia, and they had their young child, a
beautiful tousle-haired boy, in front of them; he squinted at
the camera. His wife wore a Villager skirt and blouse, and L L
Bean loafers. They were happy, centered in a tradition of the
earth that gave them sustenance, reality and meaning. It
rained, they had flowers, and harness glowed in the old
ramshackle barn, in the upper part of which was his writing
studio, and hers, since she wrote, too. There were some
quiet meditative paintings on the walls in there, and braided
rugs on the floor. An old grandfather clock ticked in the hall
of the house; bees buzzed in the heavy summer, and the
wind blew leaves, scurrying up the driveway in late autumn.
Their cheeks were red and healthy, and he ran five miles
every other day.

There was no bath in the place, and he went across town
twice a week to shower at Melanie's. The building shook with
the constant rumbling of traffic and a rock band practised at
seemingly irregular hours down below. He wrote here, and his
face was pasty urban white in the photo, with dark circles
under his eyes and visible lines on either side of his nose,
digging in, furrowing his face. He thought he could feel the
cockroaches at night in his hair. But he had gone to a good

school and served in the Marines and would go on.

The picture was taken on the campus; there was an old stone facade blooming traceries of ivy behind him. Why not here? He didn't teach here, but he had given a workshop there. There were lots of birds, a lake, and the terrific scent of youth. He smiled cryptically in the shot.

He had not graduated from the University of the Pacific but he had attended it for three months and two days. His teeth were false, and gleamed wonderfully in the picture; his custom hairpiece was an excellent job. Someone suggested he wear a hat, or a cap, like a gangster, or a sportsman, but he declined. He didn't know how to ride, but had an equestrian picture taken. In another — they wanted to have a good, full selection — he posed in a Woolrich hunting jacket, with a Golden Lab. In a third, indoor shot he was seated at his typewriter, toying with a pencil, looking as if he was just answering a question.

The picture was of him in the bar, one he never went to. Soft focus, and him looking pensive, a profile. An obviously beautiful young woman sat nearby, looking at him. He had his shirt open at the throat, and sleeves rolled up on muscular arms. There was another they took, at night, in the blaze of neon lights, wet pavements, his face half in shadow, a lonely figure.

He had a lot of friends, so they had it outside a bookstore and you had to figure out which one he was. He had never been in that bookstore and they drove him there; he was drunk, and not actually in the picture. They put in an insert of him as a cute baby.

No picture was published, saving it for the book reviews, magazine pieces, and International Famous Agency, Inc.

He was a writer, and had his picture taken through the rain flecked window of a limousine, at an international airport; a cab at a hotel, a newspaper rolled under his arm. He was a writer, and had his book jacket photo air-brushed. He was a writer and had his photo taken looking out over a lake, the sea, mountains, mist. He was a writer, and had his picture taken in a room of an old yellow stone house, with an Oriental scroll behind him, and a signet ring on his finger.

THE POET

They locked all the doors, and bathrooms. A painful evening. Eleven hundred and thirty six variations on "The dog bites the man". Interstices of the language, there where the impedimenta of breathing are not. Saw a Chinese grinning from behind a row of hung-up ducks, cleaver in his hand.

So many people in the room for the reading. The reading! Jesus! Atchinson is reading at The Terminal Cafe. Julia Harris is reading at The Calliope. Ernesto Lewis is at The Grand Piano, and Lulu Simmons Poole, the *same* night, at the Baker Street Station. Also Paul Borden is at the Five Days Bar and Grille, reading with The Accustatones. Donna Emenhizer will read her works on the radio, FM. And Rolf Rupprecht is at the Gay Dog two nights in the same week, the second a benefit for Scott Younkin. That should be a night. Marybeth Krauser is doing prose/breath performance at The Artichoke. She was just down in L. A., and then she read at Sacramento State, and did a workshop, 'Acting Out Poetry'.

Ron Savidge is going to discuss his linguistic theories of prosodic monotony, memorization, and montage; he received a government grant this year. That's at 90 De Haro Street. Bad transportation up there — got to wait a fucking hour for that bus. They shouldn't have these things up there.

Fenway Park in Boston is too small for a major league team.

Poetry of Ninety Six Nations. That's a three-day marathon reading, and there is free child care (Tot Watch) available. It's at This.

There's Max Sirardot; heavy into chant poetry. Recent reading was accompanied by Tahitian dancers. A tremendous thing. They did his play *Where Wolf,* at Laguna Gardens last month; missed it. And he sent out a card too. Must have lost it.

Everybody sends out cards, cards of their readings. Mostly these are in your various colors, because there are so many white cards in the mail. They get mixed up with the announcements of openings, art openings.

Openings, and readings. People with three names have power names. Sylvia Harris Moore. Robert John Tinker. People with only two names have just names. People with one name are entertainers.

Amy Lesher is back in town. She'd gone back to Wisconsin, but came back. It was too cold; nobody had enough money to pay for oil. She was unemployed, then made props for a mime troupe, worked on a dairy farm, and wrote poems in between.

Cop movies on TV. Black belt karate. L.A. Kung Fu. Mrs. Pimp's. A certain kind of romanticism is disgusting.

Are you going to take it? What about it? George Eliot's writing an epic poem, and will not change his name; why should he? Up in his apartment, he has Jungian stones, emblems of the self, in many locations. They are intriguing, there.

The stone is a poem!

Be a poet, and wear a Navy pea jacket, scarf, engineer boots, and walk around. Drink French Roast coffee, Mayacamas wine, Kirin beer, unblended Scotch, pernod, strawberry daiquiris, and pina coladas. Smoke Gauloises cigarettes. Eat spaghetti and clams at Baby Joe's, behind steamed windows; everybody looks in at you. A vegan lives above the deli.

There's fog in the streets tonight. When they finally broke down the bathroom door, they found an outsized gerbil who'd memorized the graffiti; it forthwith ran amok and is still loose in the city.

Just got a flyer in the mail! Bill Jones is at The Patch next week. Says he was executed at the University of Southern California and Colgate.

DR. BO

Where he got his doctorate no one could say, but everyone called him that. Jerry Lyghtens had gone down to the Deaf Club, on Valencia Street, to hear a couple of new groups The Dead Kennedys, and Little Cripples, and that's where he first saw the man. He was well known all over the area, though; some people used to proverbially set their watches (which were strictly interior) by his appearance at The Meat Market, on Noe Street. He always played a game or two of chess there in the afternoons while sipping numerous cups of espresso, wiping his copious dark beard with the back of his hand, his loud guffaws audible out in the street if the door was open. Dogs who hung out there used to prick up their ears at that laugh. Jerry became fascinated with the man — you know how it is when something like that sets in; you can't seem to do much about it. That was the way it was.

Jerry might have also been interested in the name — Bo. His own name was always being commented on, and he was tired of explaining its Dutch origin to people. He did not himself look Dutch . . . but then, what does a Dutchman look like? A long, sliding jaw, with a rather protuberant forehead, and set-in eyes? Jerry looked like a foot-ball player, with a wide pair of shoulders tapering to the slim waist of the athlete and he walked with the springy walk of athletes. He had thick, extremely curly black hair which he thought looked, if anything, either Semitic or Greek; definitely Mediterranean. His green eyes — they further confused the whole picture; they were set too wide apart, and were too large. They gave Jerry's face a look of slight astonishment, a look that some people interpreted as one of below average intelligence. Jerry also breathed with his mouth slightly open and this increased the impression, at least to some people, of possible mental deficiency. All such impressions were totally wrong, to make for the final confusion

Lyghtens worked with two other young men, making fine grade papers for artists and graphic illustrators. Their shop was located in an old warehouse on the outskirts of the Mission District; they had obtained it for a ridiculous price from the half-blind landlady/owner, an old crone who could not speak English. Her son, Carlos, a typical machismo Latino with swarthy skin and greasy black hair had negotiated for her, thinking that he was very clever. It was a good deal.

The warehouse had been found just in time, Jerry had often reflected. Now the trend was to have chic people move into these warehouses, redecorate them, and rent them out at treble and quadruple the rent that should have been obtained. Nothing like sitting in your artist's studio, looking out over China Basin, with a glittering view of the Bay Bridge at night! With a fireplace installed, the floor resurfaced, sanded, and buffed to a thick, rich gleam, a proper off-white sofa and chairs, metal tubing and glass tables, and the omni-present sound system, it was an ideal place to do dope in, and play roles. Great theater, Jerry thought. He was himself wondering how he could find a small building and start in on this business. He had seen photos in the Chronicle of a man who lived in a mansion in Pacific Heights, filled with five hundred odd teddy bears; this same person had come West, following Greeley's dictum, from Brooklyn and made millions in real estate. Now he apparently collected teddy bears, in California.

The paper-making business . . . it was going okay. Of course, it was only for a while. He could not see himself making paper for the rest of his life. In fact, he could not see himself doing anything for the rest of his life, and that was *really* the problem! One of the main reasons he had started hanging around Dr. Bo had been that he, Bo, had an aura of having successfully answered this nagging question, a question that would not go away, but that became especially persistent in the night, when one's defenses were lulled by the false security of sleep. More than once, Jerry had bolted erect in his bed in the loft, screaming. Theodore said it was just probably some bad grass, but Jerry knew this was not so. It was his dreams, and something else. Nobody seemed to talk about it, though. A taboo subject, a downer. 'Depressing!' Theodore would say. 'Let's do some more smoke. That'll fix ya up.'

Meanwhile the paper-making machine clumped on with its weird sounds, interspersed by the strangely blending-in sounds of E.J.'s saxophone playing. E.J. played at no particular time, but always seemed to prefer playing in accompaniment to this machine. It was amazing how the sounds would merge. People coming in to buy paper had sometimes even thought that E.J.'s music came from the machine. The three young men stood around the shop in their down ski jackets and construction boots; it was like a uniform they wore.

Dr. Bo seemed to have no definite age, although there were many rumors about this. Jerry had heard many of these; sitting in the Meat Market he had overheard snatches of things as Dr. Bo made his triumphal entrances. Some reputed him to be in his seventies; an 'old Wobbly, or something', Jerry overhead one man say. Others said he was in his forties, and he had even been given the distinction of being placed in that wondrous category 'the late thirties'; in other words, still young although pushing it. Dr. Bo looked quite vigorous; his skin was tanned and taut, with a fine web of lines around the eyes when he smiled, which was very often. 'Fucking grinning idiot!' was another remark Jerry had overheard in the Meat Market. He was a tall man, who had to stoop slightly as he entered doors; he had an extremely long nose, thick and heavy, that looked as if it had been set crookedly on his face. A thick, full, dark beard came down onto his chest; his hair was long and blondish — maybe bleached out by the sun. He was reputed to walk a lot in the park, and out at the beach, but Lyghtens hadn't

seen him in either place — he really hadn't looked that hard
either. Dr. Bo's voice was one of the most amazing things
about him; it was deep and sonorous and rich and he spoke
in almost cadences at times. He was wiry and obviously
quite powerful physically; nobody 'messed' with him. Jerry
had seen him walking alone at three in the morning in the
Hayes Valley area, very nonchalantly, yet vigorous and alert.
That was one of the things about him — he was 'mellow', as
the phrase had it several years back, but he also appeared
extremely keen, alert, sharp, even intense. The way he
leaned over his table as he drank his espresso, reading a
book or paper, was a good example; he looked about to
spring into the pages, like a panther. An intense air of
concentration was palpable around him; he seemed to blot
out the surroundings and people around him. This pissed
some off, for they would obviously bump against his table,
or even step on his booted foot at times, grinning instantly
and saying 'Ohh, 'scuse me, man! I didn't see where I was
goin'. Sorry.' Or something along those lines. Dr. Bo would
look up — a flick, no more — and then back to his reading.
He played chess with the same quiet ferocity.

Dr. Bo never paid his income tax, or tax of any sort that
he could avoid. Finally he led a rally against taxes. This took
place in City Hall Square, or as some called it, United
Nations Plaza. Years before, in 1946, to be precise, the
United Nations had been founded in a small, dark
auditorium across the street, that was known as the War
Memorial Veterans' Auditorium. Lyghtens had gone there
once to hear a drunken poet read his works; half-way
through, the poet had lurched from the stage, spewing
vomit. The audience had cheered, and it was considered an
event that one should not have missed.

Lyghtens attended the rally to hear Dr. Bo but got there
after he spoke, which pissed him mildly. He himself was
involved in the counterfeiting of Italian currency. This was
being done by an artist of national repute, who decided he
wanted to make the paper and make the money. It was a
statement of some sort about money. When the old janitor

came in to clean up the building one night, he found them all around the press downstairs, with the sheets of money coming off. He stared, put his fingers to his lips then, and crept out.

At the rally, though, Jerry did meet Benwhiler. Benwhiler was known only by this last name, and nobody even ever called him Ben, or Whiler, though Jerry thought those would be better names. The name business was an involved game in the city, for people changed their names continually, especially in the groups Jerry moved in. Thus nobody really believed that someone's name was what they were told, but instead upon being introduced, would nod, smile knowingly, or make some sort of facial tic to show that they 'knew'. Or they would say

'Far out, man. Glad to meet you.'

Another stock response often heard was

'Oh — neat!'

And some said

'Outta sight! Fuckin' outta sight! Space city, man, eh?'

Some said nothing; in fact, it would be this category that was probably most numerous, Jerry thought. Thus, no one *remembered* anyone else's name, either, or they confused it with someone else's; sometimes, days later, one would hear an insistent voice in one's ear on the bus, calling, or whispering, a name; one would find that an individual was staring intently at you, saying this name. The best thing to do then was simply shake one's head.

For a long time, having just one name had been considered cool. People were known as Goon, Vegetable, Bear, Gut, Fuckhead, Submarine, Ears, or Sally, and so on. This caused problems though, when trying to look people's numbers up in the phone book, and Jerry came to wonder if there were not some tricky method in this system whereby people disguised their phone numbers from unwanted callers. After all, there were many of the latter. It was said that there were always 'creeps' who attended parties, and hung out in cafes and bars, just in hope of overhearing someone's number, so that they could call them later. So it all made sense really, if you could think of it in that way and get the total picture, the full gestalt.

This was not the end of it though, for Jerry had also discovered that there were many listings in the phone books that could not possibly be real people's names. There was, for instance, the famous listing of Donald Duck. If this was really a person, then he must have had problems, Jerry reflected. But a friend pointed out that *probably* it was a *code name*. What happened here, was that you would tell people 'Oh, look, when you're in the city, see, just look up D. Duck. Call that number; you'll get me.'

This allowed of certain possibilities; for instance, that the number was actually a ruse and that the person giving it out was trying to confuse people. He/She was not actually D. Duck, and did not live there; in fact, had never heard of D. Duck, and even if they had, what kind of name was that anyway? Who would believe such a name? Really! It could also be that a nasty type would just like to sucker naive people into calling this unfortunate person, who actually *was* D. Duck, and plaguing them with all sorts of ridiculous calls and requests.

'Don't you remember me? We met in that place down in Anaheim? It was so nice!'

So it would go, with appropriate squawks on the other end.

Jerry, who had often sat in front of the phone about to dial D. Duck's number, had further thought that it might be a CIA front-type operation. They would do something like that. It might be a dumb doper's connection number, or a smart one's. It could be a call girl, or the opener to a call girl, or a house of ill repute. He never called the number, and never knew anyone who did.

There were a number of numbers like that, once you became aware of it. The phone book was 'fuckin' incredible!', as Theodore said, as they read it one night after a good smoke session. Theodore's favorite was one Dong Long, over which he nearly aspirated a pickle he was eating. There was also a listing for the HMS Bounty. It made you wonder, what was really in the phone book? It just wasn't what it appeared to be.

For these reasons, Jerry had an unlisted number.

Benwhiler had approached him in his usual fashion, tapping him on the shoulder and saying,

'Are you an eater of English muffins, my man? A drinker of the cursed potent tea?' And so on.

They went to the Museum of Modern Art cafe to get coffee, since neither of them drank tea. Benwhiler, in fact, hated tea, and hectored anyone and everyone he could about it. It was, he would say bruisedly, when someone complained about the ridiculousness of this, 'Simply a mild mania, my man. Very mild. Can't you permit me my manias? Isn't that why we all live here, together, in the city? Huh? So we can be permitted our mild manias and the free indulging of them, so long as we do not hurt others? I mean, we are all fuckin' adults are we not, eh?'

People usually left before all this was said, though, and Benwhiler would shrug, and say

'Just another goddam muffin eater. Probably with bacon, too. The fuckin' sodium nitrate. baby! That'll get ya!'

He would yell the latter after the departing people.

In the cafe they met Dr. Bo. He had apparently come there after making his speech, and was eating a huge piece of layered Viennese torte. This rather amazed Jerry. Benwhiler further amazed him by immediately marching over and squatting down on a chair by Dr. Bo.

'How ya doin', ya old shitface?' he said, pulling out from under his serape (he always wore a serape, Jerry reflected) a large brown, crumpled bag. From this he took a bright yellow banana.

'Yum, yum!' Benwhiler said, smacking his bearded lips noisely. People in the cafe looked at him uneasily.

'Potassium' he said, biting off a huge chunk.

Dr. Bo laughed, shoving the torte in his cave-like mouth, rimmed with his beard. This caused Benwhiler to begin to laugh, but he choked, and spat banana on the table. Several people got up and began to leave. Jerry hunched his shoulders and made a quick sweep of the table with a napkin. Dr. Bo pounded Benwhiler heartily on the back.

'Take it slow, man,' Jerry said. He felt uneasy in a double sense; over Benwhiler's actions, and over the meeting with Dr. Bo, who now examined him quite openly, looking him up and down. He nodded at Benwhiler.

'You know this guy?'

Jerry nodded, and sniffed loudly through his nose, for some reason he himself could not figure.

'Yeah. We went to college together. Back in Iowa.'

'Thas' right, Dr. Bo,' Benwhiler assented, and then started coughing, his face reddening. At this minute, the Prussian-looking manager of the cafe suddenly was standing at the table.

'I'm sorry, but you are not permitted to eat your lunch in the cafe,' he said, pointing to Benwhiler's brown bag, and frowning. The manager was bald, and his head glistened with a slight film of sweat. He obviously was nervous.

'What?' said Benwhiler, looking up. He swallowed loudly.

'What'd he say, man?' he asked, looking at Dr. Bo, and then Jerry.

'There is a sign. A notice.' The manager pointed outside the door.

'Isn't this a cafeteria? A place to eat your lunch?' Dr. Bo said then, leaning back expansively in his chair. He picked at his cake-crumbed beard, and examined a crumb between his large, heavy-knuckled fingers.

'Right! Right on, man!' Benwhiler roared, waving the half-bitten banana.

'Your own lunch, no. One you buy here, yes.' The manager now squared his shoulders, and drew in a breath. He straightened his white apron, and his nose twitched as if he smelled an unpleasant odor. 'So, I am afraid that I will have to ask you gentlemen to leave. If you don't mind?' He gestured toward the door.

'You fuckin' tea drinker!' Benwhiler spluttered, standing up. 'Who the hell are you, anyway?'

Dr. Bo stood, and touched Benwhiler lightly on the shoulder. The manager had backed up several paces. A white-garbed cook emerged from the kitchen behind the counter; a large, burly man, with a bloody apron on.

'Hans!' the manager hissed. The cook approached.

'We were just leaving,' Dr. Bo said. He turned to Benwhiler. 'After you.'

Hans puffed up to the table. He was remarkably porcine-looking, and his eyes glinted from face to face. The tall chef's hat teetered on his thick head.

'Don't *breathe* on me, you schweinhund! Benwhiler said. He had taken German in college, to the dismay of many of the language faculty.

'Gentlemen, please!' the manager said.

They left then, Jerry slurping his coffee and burning his tongue. Benwhiler, in the elevator, lunged his head out before the doors closed.

'Fuckin' Nazis! Sieg Heil!' He clicked his sneakers, and gave a Fascist salute that nearly was caught in the closing doors.

They adjourned to McDonald's, where they got coffees and sat out on the upstairs deck, in the fresh, ever-remarkable California sunlight. Dr. Bo chuckled; Jerry thought he was one of the few people he had ever heard who really did that. And it sounded good too, in his deep voice; it was somehow comforting. Benwhiler fumed. He had done a goose-step out of the elevator and on out of the museum, until he had stepped in dogshit and fell off the edge of a curb crossing Ellis Street, thus very nearly being run over by a speeding Datsun 280Z, driven by a startled-looking young Chinese wearing thick-lensed, wire-rimmed glasses.

'Fuckin' Chinese porno film director, no doubt!' Benwhiler had yelled. He had limped to McDonald's, cursing 'the fuckin' facists, man; they're everywhere now. You can't go in a goddamn museum; there's some damn ex-Prussian drillmaster cum Nazi bastard in there. Herr Direktor! This country's goin' to the *dogs*, man; I tell you.'

Dr. Bo, occasionally supporting Benwhiler, seemed to

enjoy it all. People looked at them as they entered McDonald's, but the place was located in a heavy combat zone of the inner city, so the looks were not too long. One saw many types there, daily. It was a strange McDonald's, as those ubiquitous eateries go, for it was very well-appointed for such an area of the city. Further, it covered nearly the entire block, which made it the largest McDonald's Jerry could remember ever seeing, or being in.

'I heard you were counterfeiting,' Dr. Bo said quietly, as they sat there. Benwhiler and Jerry both blinked in the bright sun reflecting from the metal and glass of the McDonald's dome, which Benwhiler had pointed to suddenly, and said 'They ripped that off, man! Took it right from Buckminster Fuller. Look at it!'

Jerry was so surprised he took too large a gulp of coffee to cover his confusion, and again burned his tongue. He coughed, and his eyes watered.

'Let's go to Mexico, Dr. Bo,' Benwhiler urged, leaning across the coughing Jerry. 'Let's go on down into the *real* jungle — let's go on down to Guatemala! They say there's a good train takes you down there in a couple a days, pretty cheap fare an' all.'

'I don't want to travel on any cheap Central American train,' Dr. Bo said, looking off somewhere behind Benwhiler.

A look of recognition flashed on Benwhiler's face. He seized Jerry's arm, thus spilling most of the coffee from Jerry's cup onto his Levis. Jerry winced, shutting his eyes.

'Hey! Look! This guy here — sorry about that, man, Jesus, are you okay?' He peered intently at Jerry who nodded his head, clenching his teeth.

'Ain't you doin' money? Didn't I hear you say that?'

'Italian money. Lira. It's only an art project.'

'Lira?'

'That's the Italian currency,' Dr. Bo explained to Benwhiler, who made an 'Ooh' with his lips, and peered around him covertly.

'That's cool. Let's go over to Italy then. You know, I

always wanted to get back over to Europe, anyway.'
Benwhiler smiled. 'I can dig it.'

'Where were you? In Europe?' Jerry asked. He had the
feeling that Benwhiler was crazy, but dismissed the thought
as unworthy.

'I was over there, all over. Couple a years back — four or
five years ago. I went to Denmark. You ever been there?'

Jerry shook his head. He did not want to talk of this, he
realized. He turned to Dr. Bo, and blurted it out.

'Listen . . . can you tell me . . . can you give me any
idea . . .'

'Let's go to Ireland, man! I hear you don't pay any taxes
there, huh?'

'Only for creative artists,' Dr. Bo said. He had rolled a
cigarette, and now lit it. He looked expectantly at Jerry.

' . . . how I should live my life?' Jerry concluded. He
blushed, and looked down at the cement floor.

'Yeah, well . . . there's some island over there, near there,
and the people don't pay a fuckin' cent of tax. Nothin!
That's the place to go . . . except it's so damn cold over
there. I saw this movie about some place in England; it was
rainin' all the time.'

'The Isle of Man,' Dr. Bo said. 'That's the place where
they pay no tax. Some sort of old feudal agreement.'

Benwhiler stood up and looked around, hands on hips.
Then he sat down. 'Yeah, well, the main thing is to get outta
this place. This fuckin' country! I'm fed up with it. Fed up,
to here!' He made a motion with his hand over his head, and
leered out from under it.

'How often do you feel like this?' Dr. Bo asked, smiling.
He patted Jerry on the shoulder at the same time. Jerry felt
he'd received his answer, and took a deep breath, relaxing.

'Oh, yeah!' Benwhiler said, twisting his mouth in a sneer.
'I can see the drift of your thought. Sure. Five or six times a
day — that's how often. At *least* that often!'

Dr. Bo raised his eyebrows. 'Serious,' he said, exhaling a
little smoke.

When Jerry got back to the warehouse and told them he

was leaving, E.J. and Theodore did not have much to say.
On the way home, Benwhiler had told him that Dr. Bo had
assisted a friend of his who had fallen in love with a
computer; a technological encounter, he termed it.
Benwhiler said that he felt that some chemical of
unhappiness was active in him; he suspected that the
government might even be releasing this gradually into the
populace in selected areas, into the water and air, as a mood
control experiment. He elaborated on this, and said that in
his case the chemical, which was supposed to make people
placid and mild, had the reverse effect upon him. He was
happy that Jerry and he and Dr. Bo had agreed to meet at
the airport and light out for someplace else. He put a strong
emphasis on the word *else*, pounding his fist in his palm.

'The territory ahead! That's it, man!' Benwhiler said, his
eyes glistening.

They had decided upon no place in particular and had
agreed that Dr. Bo would announce the selection once they
all arrived at the airport, later that night. They each had a
few hours to pack. It was the kind of thing that happened
daily in San Francisco, Jerry knew. When he had left Iowa
for the coast, a close friend and his 'steady' girl (who later
got married in Chicago) told him not to go, saying 'It's a *zoo*
out there, Jerry! I've been there — nobody has any roots,
nobody cares about anything! The weather's too nice; it's
too comfortable!'

Back at the warehouse, E.J. was running the machine and
Theodore was reading a book, and neither of them said too
much when Jerry said he was leaving.

'Just for a while, you know . . .'

'Sure,' said E.J.

'What's that book?' Jerry asked Theodore, who he felt
was less happy over his leaving. He felt a need to make some
conversation — things could get too cool, after all.

'*The Dragons of Eden,* by Carl Sagan' Theodore said, not
looking up.

E.J. shut off one part of the machine to cut down the
noise level. 'Science fiction, eh? Eh, Theodore?' he said,

grinning.

'It's about the *brain*, man, the human *brain*,' Theodore answered, sitting up from the position he had been in. He stretched himself in his down jacket.

'No shit?' marveled E.J.

'Ahhh . . .' Theodore said, shaking his head.

'You never know what people are readin' these days,' E.J. said to Jerry. 'People are really gettin' into readin again, you know? That's good for us, too. In fact, there was a guy over here from the West Coast Print Center the other day, about some fine paper book job, some number he had . . . you know those people have a government grant?'

Joe Filbert came in as Jerry was finishing packing. He was a student at UC Berkeley, and worked part time in a bakery near the warehouse. He accosted Jerry as he was leaving.

'Did you see my contact lens case? I think I left it over here.'

E.J. held it up — a small, grey piece of plastic. Jerry nodded his head at both of them, and left. Theodore was still reading *The Dragons of Eden*. Outside, Jerry stopped for a minute; the heavy thump-thump of the paper-maker could be heard, and felt. The old warehouse loomed above him. He liked it — the oldness of it. He liked that best, he decided.

On his way to the airport, he had many thoughts; they all passed in front of him as if on a screen. He felt rather numb. Coming past a parked car downtown, walking to the airlines bus terminal, he saw a redhead lighting a cigarette in a grey car, with the door partly open. She looked at him evenly, exhaling a small wisp of smoke, with a slight smile. She had legs like cream. Jerry shook his head and walked faster towards the terminal. The whole city's like that, he thought. He wondered why he did not go back, talk to her. He wondered what Dr. Bo would have done.

Out at the airport, Benwhiler was in a dither. Jerry saw him pacing back and forth, through the glass doors that open and shut automatically. He raced across the terminal floor, brandishing a newspaper, people looking askance at him.

'Look at this!' Benwhiler said, shoving the ragged paper under Jerry's nose. 'A ring of international drug traffickers buying ergot in West Germany, where it's legal, and bringing it here, where it's made into acid. Worth 48 million fuckin' dollars on the street! The ringleaders are all *judo masters* — Jesus, can you believe this shit, man! — all judo masters who studied in Tokyo together some fourteen years ago. The ergot was smuggled into the United States in judo mats.'

Jerry sat down in a seat facing a large plate glass window looking out on the taxiing planes. He shook his head; Benwhiler threw up his hands, and pitched the paper into the vacant chair next to him.

'Well . . . that's the way it goes these days,' Jerry said, feeling asinine.

'That's nothing, man,' Benwhiler said, indicating the paper with a jab of his finger. 'There's a piece in there about the Queen of England's limousine being hit by three gypsies. Fuckin' scrap dealers, over in England.'

'What?' Jerry felt slightly shocked.

'And in the same paper, another article about this guy back east, who had his dick cut off in a hospital — shit, can you imagine *this!* This old doctor cut off this guy's dick — *by mistake!*' Benwhiler closed his eyes in a painful grimace, and clutched himself. 'Uhhhh!'

'Come on, man,' Jerry exclaimed, sitting up in his chair.

'True, true; all of it true. Honest to God!' Benwhiler raised his hand solemnly, as if taking an oath. Then he seized the paper, and thrust it into Jerry's midsection. 'Fuck — read it yourself, then.'

Jerry shook his head, and placed the paper, which he tried to fold up neatly, in the chair beside him.

Benwhiler was looking over the crowded interior of the airport, moving restlessly in his chair.

'I've been tryin' to leave this city for ten years now. But I've never been able to do it . . . never been able, nope. No way. Something always comes up — you know.'

Jerry nodded. The smell of jet fuel mixed with excessive cigarette smoke made him slightly nauseous. Benwhiler's fidgeting did not make it any better.

'Hey! Let's go up to Oregon, and buy Pendleton shirts, and penny loafers. Argyle socks. Be casual, look like golfers.' Benwhiler laughed loudly, and slapped Jerry on the back. 'Ehhh?' Then he stopped laughing, and took a deep breath.

'You know, coming out here tonight, I finally figured out something.' He paused expectantly, looking at Jerry.

'What?' Jerry asked politely.

Benwhiler then launched into a long description of the smell of the city, which he said had always baffled him, tantalized him, for years. This smell, he announced loudly, was sex. The whole city reeked of it, he crowed. Then he said that it was strange that an entire city should smell so sexy, but that it was *true*, that it was not an illusion; he was now certain of it. Leaving on their trip, he said, had already sharpened his senses.

'How do you know it's not an illusion?' Jerry asked, not knowing what he was actually saying. He was always polite, and responded.

Benwhiler sat erect as if stabbed.

'How?! What difference does it make — if it's baloney, an illusion, anyway? It's all we have — I don't mean just the sex thing now; I mean the whole damn smear. The works. It's all we have. So we ought to throw ourselves into it, and enjoy it. Right? We might come out the other side, and find we got the real thing!'

'Where's Dr. Bo? Jerry asked then, looking around. 'He should be getting here.'

Benwhiler suddenly looked tired and flopped back into his chair. He lit a cigarette. Then he was pushing something — the matches — into Jerry's face.

'Jesus, will you quit shoving shit in my face?'

'No, man — I mean, *look* at this!'

It was a box of matches.

They were finely made, and were from Italy. They were in

a square little box, with a picture in color of the Lake of
Como on one side, and of the Duomo in Milan on the other.

Benwhiler sighed as Jerry handed the matches back,
nodding.

'They even make their matches beautiful, attractive.
Maybe we ought to go there — you were doin' that lira
money, you said.'

'That was something different. That was an art thing. I
told you about that, before.'

Benwhiler nodded. 'Yeah . . . art. Hey, I wonder where it
is old Dr. Bo decided we should go? I was thinkin' about
that too comin' out here. I heard he went down to the
Amazon not too long ago, you know. I hear it's fuckin'
unbelievable down there. Unbelievable! A paradise!'

'Maybe so,' Jerry said. He did not know if he wanted to go
to the Amazon, at least not at that point in his life. 'What
would we do down there?'

'Huh? Whadda ya mean, do?'

'I don't speak Spanish,' Jerry explained.

'Oh, hell, they all speak English! Don't you know that?
Why, the world —'

Benwhiler's name was being paged. He looked around
him wide-eyed, and then grabbed Jerry by his down jacket.
Jerry had been thinking he would not need it in the Amazon.

'Hey — listen! That's me they want!'

They both went to the message counter together. The
clerk, an attractive efficient young woman in a tailored blue
suit, gave them a small white sheet of paper. Benwhiler
unfolded it, and read it aloud.

'Go back to Iowa. Go home. Dr. Bo.'

'Shit!' Benwhiler exclaimed sharply. He lunged over the
counter towards the clerk, who backed quickly away from
him.

'Is this all there is? This is all the message there is?'

'Yes sir,' the startled clerk said, in a high voice. 'That's the
message. There wasn't anything else.'

Benwhiler raised his arms skyward and then threw the
crumpled note on the smooth waxed floor.

'Can you believe it? Damn! Didn't I tell you?' He kicked at the small, white ball of paper, then trod on it, slipping, almost falling.

'That's all this place is — fuckin' paper! The whole goddamn world is nothin' but paper!' he yelled wildly. Jerry took his arm, and they walked away from the counter, where the clerk was edging nearer to a telephone, eyeing them.

Benwhiler fell suddenly silent. They walked quietly back over to where they had been sitting before. They sat there for a couple of minutes, neither saying anything. Benwhiler heaved a large sigh twice, shaking his head. Jerry felt swaddled and muffled in his down jacket; his face felt numb. Everything around him looked sharp, distinct.

Benwhiler turned to him. 'Let's have us an Irish in the bar, since we're out here . . . watch the planes take off. Couple times I've come out here, just to do that.'

The big planes' lights shone wetly on the taxiways outside the long window. They went inside the bar called The Tahitian Lounge, where a fresh-faced collegiate girl, in what looked like a real grass skirt, smiled at them as they entered, and said

'Gentlemen.'

A BOWL OF SOUP

To be attacked by a bowl of soup might be considered a strange fate. And yet such was the case with my friend Klipstein; indeed, we can say it has altered his entire life, although Klipstein himself is the type of man whose character and real motivations in life were and are always in dispute among his associates. Some men are born great, others attain greatness, and still others have greatness foisted, as it were, upon them, Klipstein was and is one whom others suspect of some unknown, even mysterious, form of greatness, but which has yet to manifest itself in the great world in some form of what is generally termed success.

For in all truth, Wolfgang Jovanovitch (such are his forenames to which he clings assiduously, even ruthlessly and in fact, will brook no abbreviation of, except among his closest intimates) had what appeared to be a most usual sort of life. A clerk in the offices of the Sierra Railway Company for some fifteen years or more, he presents, and to my knowledge has never presented differently, a most ordinary outward appearance. Of course, everyone knows someone of their acquaintance like Klipstein; undistinguished in externals but in some ill-defined and perhaps not often enough studied fashion, manifesting uniqueness.

And to proceed quickly, Klipstein, once known, was much different than any casual acquaintanceship could have possibly conveyed. When I first came to know him, it was already difficult to adjudge his actual age, since he himself gave the most confusing statements about it and would in no way answer a direct question concerning his years, his birthday, or even his birthplace. At various times, I myself believed him to be of my own age, roughly forty-three or so. However an associate once assured me, with vehemence, that Klipstein was nearly sixty and was a war veteran; indeed, that he had even received a high military decoration. This, I must say, was difficult to believe — I mean, that he was that old — since he was, of all things, a man of surpassing physical vigor. Take for example his widely known walking tours. These consisted of strolls, as he termed them, that might in the course of a day encompass a good part of the city limits! But these were nothing compared to his near-legendary hikes in remote areas. It was reported by one young man in the office that Klipstein had been known to walk a certain mountain trail, the length of which I could never clearly ascertain exactly, in his week's vacation in the summer; the young man himself had it that motor conveyances had been used in this feat, for otherwise it was beyond credence. However, as to this latter, I know for a fact beyond all question that Klipstein had a pronounced loathing of cars, buses and especially motorcycles; often I heard him curse these vehicles aloud in the street, to the amazement of other pedestrians and the embarrassement of myself. He would at these times deliver a loud harangue, stopping and waving his arms agitatedly, which could produce an odd spectacle. No, seriously, it is to be doubted if he would have even come near such transport in his solitary hikes, especially since I have the distinct impression that these events were of an almost religious nature to him. Perhaps more amazing were reports that he had at one time walked the entire length of England from John O'Groats to Land's End. This was quite believable to me though, for he possessed a passion, a real love in fact, for all things English, and the only real peculiarity of outward nature one could fairly ascribe to him was his preference for an English style of clothing, which he purchased faithfully in the same shop at selected times of every year.

So at this point, it is only fair to say that no one knew or knows, the precise age of Klipstein but, as for that, reflecting upon it, we could say that it may not in the last analysis matter. Or, at least, very little. Actually I can say myself, that although for a period of time I was rather curious even somewhat intrigued by this chronological question, it soon ceased to occur to me and finally, I believe it ceased to have any interest at all for me. Yet one cannot help wondering what he, Klipstein, thought of it and the event I tell of here may have been, in some obscure way, to him at least, a revelation in this respect.

I have said that certain facts of life, as they might be termed, were, and still are to my knowledge, unavailable concerning my friend. His nationality, a common topic, excited much speculation in our office since he spoke with an accent — and yet, *what kind* of accent was it? And from where? A number of people assumed him to be Jewish, no doubt due to his name. This is easy to understand. But at various times he himself let slip, in my company, hints of another lineage. He often spoke, for instance, of the ancient Celts, and possessed a rich store of legends, tales and even words from that language. Perhaps it is possible that he is of the Celtic tribe, and he loved to tell Irish jokes. Two men in the office and a clerk in the shop where he bought his yearly allotments of clothing, swear he is a Pole. Yet, and perhaps most strange there is the indisputable fact that he speaks fluent Norwegian. If I flatter myself to think that I am his closest friend, yet it would be unfair to withhold the reality of his close attachment to an old sea captain, now retired, with whom he hob-nobbed, as he termed it, once every week or so in a dingy saloon on the waterfront. Once I accompanied him to this nautical rendezvous, an occasion which I recall even now with mixed feelings. It seemed to me that an unknown depth of experience was revealed in that dive while Klipstein and his crony smoked black cigars, drank rum and water and conversed in Norwegian. Although I had never considered him before then to be an ascetic, yet I must confess I was perplexed and finally dumfounded, as they say, at Klipstein's drinking prowess.

As I think this one example will indicate, Klipstein, once known, began to assume quite other dimensions than those of a humble clerk, responsible for bills of lading, lumber counts, boxcar numbers and other such items which constituted his daily employment. One naturally asks, as I did, how such a man could pursue such a humble and seemingly futile, meaningless profession? Quite simply, this was and remains a mystery. However, realistically speaking, it must be noted that like so many others of us, his source of monetary income was not of cardinal importance in his life. There can be little if any doubt about this, for it is well known in the office that Klipstein was a mildly sluggardly man at his duties and, in fact, often performed them rather poorly or, in several instances, not at all. I could even say that he seemed at times to take a sheer perverse delight in mismanaging his job, as witness the instance when he dispatched an order by telegraph, which he later confirmed over the phone (although he vigorously denied the latter, I am duty bound, in the interests of fairness, to say I heard or rather, over-heard him, with my own ears) to a train-loading crew which resulted in an entire shipment of lumber being lost. I mean, to be absolutely clear on this, that the said shipment never has been relocated, nor has it ever been determined if it, in fact, existed! Incredible as this must sound, the rumor that a junior clerk passed on to me I found even more remarkable, even disturbing, in a way. This was that Klipstein himself told this same clerk that he intended to 'have a bit of sport' with things; the clerk inferring, I believe, that Klipstein concocted the entire event; a total fabrication. Needless to say, the communications channels of the company were for some time badly fouled over this matter, and I myself sorely vexed, for it fell out that I was charged with unsnarling the error, which to my detriment, no doubt, I never succeeded in doing. You can now see what I mean when I say there was more to him than meets the eye. Our friendship was somewhat strained for a period following this but, strange to say, the entire business lent more of an aura of attraction to the man to me, reluctant though I am to admit it.

What, then, was his *real* profession? Of course, as I myself often suspected, many believed that he possessed independent means, or that he was merely performing his tasks, this menial, dull job to support an aged parent or loved one. I have since come to the conclusion that he did not and does not, possess that really indefinite item, 'independent means', at least in any quantifiable fashion. I say this because his ignorance, or at least apparent ignorance, of the stock market, commodities, bonds — indeed, even the rates of exchange in our own business — is nothing short of abysmal, even profound, and I would not have believed it if I had not plenteous evidence of the first hand-variety.

As to the second motive, it is difficult to know what to say. For who can believe that he never mentioned parents, or loved ones, or even distant familial relations? But such, I assure you, is the case. The Norwegian sea captain, once meeting me in a restaurant where we often ate, implied in terribly broken English that Klipstein had once been married, and even that it was a passionate union. After some two years or more, I finally was invited to visit Klipstein's lodgings, which were not in any way fantastically unique, except that he kept a large parrot which had an odd vocabulary, and that the walls of every room were lined from floor to ceiling with books. His lodging, or apartment, was in a decidedly run-down section of the city, an area I myself thought it even rather dangerous to live in. A small brass plate with W.J.K. was affixed over the bell. And it was here that I saw a photograph of a woman — perhaps his wife, his sweetheart, his sister. I hadn't the temerity to ask him, even though I could not keep my eyes from it, which he must have noticed, for he is a very keen observer of people.

However, Klipstein kept the company of women, for he was seen at the Opera at least twice with a woman. And it was a different woman on each occasion. He was convivial with women, even at times, I might say, bordering on risque.

At this point, some might say that there was and is nothing out of the ordinary here. However, reflection on the whole business as I have experienced it has led me to doubt this and to even wonder if I myself have not been decidedly altered by my contact with what appeared to be, indeed, just ordinary. And then, the fact and incident of the attack on Klipstein, which I mentioned at the beginning, has put a different light on it all, at least for me.

I forget to mention that other theories concerning Klipstein's true profession abounded. They were so numerous and so amazing that I feel bound to cite at least several in passing, remembering the average spectacle he presented to the world and marveling at the pursuits that were foisted on him through people's incredible imaginations, people who scarcely even knew much beyond his literal name. To be short then, it was bandied about that he was a criminal of various types; that he was a jewel thief, in particular. Personally, since he never wore any jewelry whatsoever on his person, and never evinced any interest at all in any sort or type of jewelry, I had to really scoff at this attribution. Imagine my amazement when this very fact was then put forth as the leading proof of his artfulness as a crook! Truly, the mind of man knows no limits and its perversity is astonishing and this incident, this vicious canard about my friend, was enough to prove it to me.

Another legend (for such they became) was that he was a writer. As some have remarked, today when persons are unsure of things, etc., they often say, in response to queries, that they are writers. It is easy for others to accept this, for everyone knows that a writer performs his work alone, unseen. One can see a painter, or photographer, or dancer at work and no mistake about it. But it is different with writers. In fact, how many secret writers are among us would be a moot question indeed. And if Klipstein may have told others that he was a writer, there still remains the question, was he an *author*? Is there not a subtle difference?

Especially among his detractors, these questions, I am afraid, were never even raised. They had it that Klipstein's literary efforts were in the production of salacious books and novels, which he would, of course, publish under a pseudonym, receiving large sums for his smutty labors. Again, it was the focusing on Klipstein's being a pornographer (for it was really nothing short of that, in so many words, minced here and there, of course) that was a grievous consternation to me. One old man in the office, to his credit, thought Klipstein was a 'scholar', although he appeared uncertain as to the nature of Klipstein's special scholarly interests. I could well believe this theory to some extent, given the glimpses I had had of his hoards of books. Yet most of the others adduced as proof of his villainies in the flesh trades the fact that he never looked at certain magazines circulated in the office, or at a calendar kept in the records vault, inside a large file cabinet. I pointed out that neither did I, at least not for any length of time, but they sneered at me.

But even more grievous to me were the rumors, which grew quite powerfully, that he was a miser and practitioner of the sin of avarice on a gigantic scale. Easy though it may have been to see some basis for such rumors, the magnitude they reached soon surpassed all bounds of decency. Certainly it is a truism, and even a hazard of a single, unmarried life, that one is suspected of possessing larger ready sums of money than one's married friends and associates, who, after all, have the expenses of raising children, buying a home, much larger medical, dental, and food expenses, and so on. Since Klipstein, to all knowledge, had neither wife, nor child, nor house, nor even a car, and as his physical vigor appeared to need no assistances, or only at best, quite minor ones, from physicians, many, I believe, not only suspected he was possessed of a private hoard of money but really envied the man. Perhaps no passion or feeling is as damaging as envy, and I believe my friend suffered quite unjustly due to it. But then, if one reflects, it could be fairly said, who has not? Yet, as was the case in other stories concerning Klipstein, it seemed no bounds existed. It was adduced by his accusers, as proof of his extreme miserliness, that he never rode the public transport, but, regardless of the weather, would be seen walking to and from the office. Although I strenuously remonstrated with the accusers on this particular charge especially, pointing out his known loathing of motor conveyances, they shook their heads at me, smiling, winking, and nodding in a curious, sage-like fashion, sometimes uttering phrases like 'A deep one, a deep one; deep waters there', and other such rather ridiculous things. The fact that he had somewhat of a passion for old silver plate was, in some ways, one of the most damning traits to his detractors and although he once explained that the cleaning and polishing of this old ware was a 'Zen exercise' of meditation for him, this explanation, as might be expected, was hooted at and derided.

Indeed, a full summary of the intricacies of his sup- posed miserly machinations, his plotting deviousness, his reputed unsavory connections in the so-called 'underworld' of finance (especially money-lending), would actually approach epic scale if I had the time or space here to recount it all in its labyrinthian twistings.

Whatever may or may not be really known of my friend can now be seen in a better light and so I will pass on to the event which was the cause of everything, at least as I see it now, in hindsight, so to speak.

For some years Klipstein took his lunch at a restaurant that was located upstairs in a large office building in the financial district of the city. He lunched here because the restaurant was inexpensive, yet the food quite palatable, especially their soups, and because there is a fine view from the windows near the table where he usually sat.

I say usually, for his habit concerning luncheons was rather strict and unvarying, at least from one viewpoint. For, although I had been his friend for a good while, I never knew from week to week if I would be his companion at lunch or not. It was his practice then to ask you to accompany him to lunch on the very morning of the meal itself, sometimes a half-hour or less before noon; at other times, he would ask you perhaps the evening before, and I should report that he did arrange with me several times a luncheon date even a week in advance. The reason for the latter occurrences I never puzzled out. I should also note that, although I have said that I imagine myself his closest friend (known to *me*, that is), Klipstein often lunched alone and with others. For example, he liked to take his noon repast (as he himself often called it) in the company of a typesetter from one of the daily newspapers, whose pressrooms were near-by. This typesetter, an Irishman of the name of Early, would bring Klipstein examples of oddities he discovered in editions of the paper; anomalies in spelling, and the like, which would result in curious, often humorous, conjunctions of words and meanings. Or, perhaps it would be more accurate to call them mis-meanings. This same Mr. Early had a wry type of wit and I learned at one luncheon that he himself occasionally set up an 'error' in the columns of the paper, which he and Klipstein would then laugh loudly over. Another fairly regular luncheon associate of Klipstein's was a tall, thin, red-haired woman named Flora whose last name I never learned. She apparently provided Klipstein with books for his library, and it was charming to see the delight with which these two would leaf through a tome she had brought to him, uttering strange little cries of excitement and pleasure that would cause the other occupants of the restaurant to even stare at them, to which they appeared oblivious.

But frequently he liked his lunch alone. I often speculated on what he did during these solitary meals. I confess, although it must be readily apparent by now, that I had, by this time, formed an intense interest in Klipstein's activities, and was even upset when he failed to ask me to lunch or informed me he 'had some things to do', by which, of course, I was to understand he wished to eat by himself. Frankly, even now, I cannot arrive at the real reasons for my feelings in this regard. It is a mystery to me; perhaps it shall ever remain so. In any case, on at least four occasions, I was so driven, I may say, by this nagging wonderment as to what he did while he ate alone, that I spied on him. Yes, I have to admit it could be called nothing else and it bewildered me that I could do such a thing to my friend. However, I soon discovered, in conversation with one of our office associates, that several others had done the same thing. But this fact did not noticeably alleviate my guilt feelings.

And what did I observe in my clandestine watchings of this man? Absolutely nothing, I must report. After he had obtained his meal, usually a soup of the day and an entree, he would seek his wonted table where he would slowly eat his lunch, usually alternating between reading some book or other he nearly always had with him and looking out the large window. Once he read a newspaper, and once he jotted something in a small, brown notebook he carried. I observed that, after his meal, with what I would have to term relish, he lit a cigarette and smoked it leisurely, looking out the window, and he did this each of the four times I watched him. This, in fact, was the only thing he did that surprised me, for I had never observed him smoking in our office at all. And I noted that he carried his cigarettes in a small metal box; I could not, however, ascertain if they were of a foreign make or not. It is certain, to me, that the box was not a common cigarette package or container, however.

All of this in some fashion disappointed me, for I thought, for what reason I cannot conceive, that he would do something quite out of the ordinary at these solitary meals. So did the others who had spied on him; their observations, however, tallied nearly exactly with mine. Perhaps we all expected some sort of rendezvous at these meals, a woman, etc. Who knows, perhaps he was, in fact, doing something unique — but none of us ever observed such.

The day of the attack was a day on which he was there alone. As far as I have been able to check, no one saw the event and it was he himself who told me of it, for it had, obviously, a profound effect upon him. Here then, is what did occur, as he told it to me, later that very afternoon.

Entering the afore-mentioned restaurant, Klipstein ordered a small bowl of chicken and rice soup and half a ham sandwich on whole wheat, with a cup of tea. He took his food to the favored table where he sat alone. After having eaten a bite or two of his sandwich, he decided to add some salt and pepper to his soup, which, he said, he suspected was 'rather torpid'. (Those were his exact words — 'rather torpid'.) Picking up the pepper shaker — he was quite certain it was the pepper, for it had made him sneeze — it slipped from his grasp, and smashed on the table, breaking apart. The pepper 'shot voluminously' (again, his words) all over the table and on his trousers. Klipstein noted that, in his opinion, the pepper shaker was greasy which made it slip out of his fingers.

He then noted, most curiously I thought, that this accident confirmed a feeling he had had all day, that 'it was not his day'. A waiter came quickly; the broken pieces of the shaker were swept from the floor, along with the pepper. Klipstein cleaned the top of the table himself, he said, with a napkin. He then proceeded with his lunch; he told me he was reading D.H. Lawrence's *Sea and Sardinia,* a travel book and enjoying it quite a bit.

He began to eat his soup; he ate at least several spoonfuls, and then it happened. As he masticated a bit of chicken, he felt a gritty substance between his molars; luckily, as he put it, he immediately stopped eating, and 'fished out', from his mouth a long, pointed sliver of what could only be — glass!

Needless to say, as he himself said, he was struck with the instant thought that he quite possibly had already, in the soup previously consumed, ingested other bits of glass and that it, this glass (from the broken pepper shaker, obviously), was even at that moment working into his stomach, and thus into his intestines.

The upshot of this was that Klipstein pushed the soup aside and ate no more of it. He did, however, finish his ham sandwich; he told me he felt the bread might counter-act the glass, if he had inadvertently eaten any. Then he left the restaurant, with some half-hour of his alloted one-hour lunch time still to go. He said he spent most of this time 'walking about downtown'.

And so the most striking event occurred; yet even more striking, certainly, was what followed. Klipstein returned to our office that afternoon, and, as far as I can tell, he sought me out immediately. I remember that he did not seem unduly agitated, but, of course, I must have been wrong. He narrated the events as I have; then he asked me what I thought of the fact that 'A man could be attacked by an anonymous bowl of soup, which has glass in it, which could *kill* him. Such is his life, do you realize that? Just like that!' So he said, snapping his fingers at the 'Just like that!'

I believe I laughed at this and said perhaps he was over-reacting. Really, I am not certain; I wish I were, for evidently, he took the whole ludicrous business quite seriously. I think I may have said that it was sort of an odd thing to have happen to one but, after all, restaurant patrons often discovered foreign substances in their food. He agreed and, smiling, left my office.

And now here is the strangest part, to my mind and, indeed, all of us in the office think so. For, apparently, not only did Klipstein leave my office; he left the office itself, his apartment and the city. Now, I ask you, can you imagine such a thing? But such is the truth of this bizarre story, for what else could it, in all justice, be termed?

Yes, he left. Where did, or where rather, has he gone? One of my hopes in writing all of this down is that he may see it and know that we all wonder about him; we miss him; we are perplexed by him and this apparently senseless action of his. I can say here, incidentally, that despite such an unprecedented departure, such an unexplained absence, the Sierra Railway Company (and I have this on the most *reliable* authority) stands ready to take him back into their employ. Certainly this is very generous, I think most would say. And no questions will be asked, I can assure you. After all, we all recognize that things do happen in life, yes, indeed. We have no wish to invade his privacy in this instance or any other, for that matter.

Such were and are the strange facts in this, what must be admitted, most strange affair of our friend Klipstein and, incredibly, a bowl of soup. I must say that the old Norwegian sea captain, whom I informed of this whole business, said he believed Klipstein had gone on a long hike into the mountains. Indeed, he did not seem upset but even,

I might say, rather happy. One man in the office persistently rumors it that Klipstein went to England, since he spoke of it so often to him. But it staggers belief that a generally competent and mature man would do such a thing. How would he live?

As for myself, I can only say that I remain in the dark and can only hope that he, Klipstein, somehow finds out that he is thought of constantly (never a day goes by in the office that he is not discussed) and missed. In fact, oddly enough, it could be said that it is true that he is here more now (in a sense) than he was when he was actually here — although, of course, he is actually missing. Ah, indeed, a strange business ! A strange business, and I wonder if we shall ever really, in fact, see the end of it. I must say, it is most upsetting, and I, for one, as I said at the beginning, could never, in all my waking days, as the saying has it, have imagined such a business. It has been some relief to me to tell it all, for such has been the effect of Klipstein's adventure, that I myself, now when I eat a bowl of soup, am constantly wondering if I might not find glass in it, too, and then what will I do?

ACE: VENICE —
THE GREAT SEAMUS

Ace: Venice is an art gallery located at 72 Market Street in Venice, California. Although Venice is actually a legal entity unto itself, a real municipality, most people immediately recognize it as being part of Los Angeles — and that has everything to do with everything. For Los Angeles — *L.A.*, as knowledgeable people style it — is the capital of fantasy, of dream-spinning, of myth-making. Modern man has revealed lately a deep hunger for myths. In contemporary advertising and films, for instance, we see small silver or gold ornaments glowing amongst the hairs of a sullen looking male model's chest. What do they signify? Truly, a mystery.

These sorts of matters were often the subjects of deep discussions in my rooms at Number 1 Enterprise Street, in San Francisco, far away to the north of Los Angeles. *Northern* California — a different country, a different state of affairs, at the very least, or so some argued and still do. Whatever one's views on that wonderful question — and it was frequently and heatedly discussed at Number 1 Enterprise — it was really another mystery, Seamus Vincent, who used to occupy center place in that loft, literally and metaphorically, and it was Seamus who was the cause of all this business that follows. He was actually a painter, although he had long since ceased to even use the phrase. He had that damn smugness of the artist, always at work, or 'working' — making you feel, inevitably, that you were a lazy, good-for-nothing; an insignificant. Personally knowing an artist often has this effect on me, I've noticed. They make you feel you're not doing anything worthwhile with your life; you're not *producing* anything, or even really experiencing anything. Life is passing you by, like a train passing a potential passenger in a station, with a thunderous purposeness and force, nearly knocking you down and taking your breath away, even scaring you. So it was with Seamus. He was actually a Southern Californian too, having been born and raised in, of all places, Ventura. One of the few things I could ever say that would make him writhe was that name Ventura. But even that fitted him in a fashion, for he was constantly travelling and often turned up in the most remote spots or the current voguish ones. He'd been to all of them twice. Seamus visited me more and more frequently, since he coveted my 'space', as he termed it, for a studio. My 'rooms' (I have always had an affection for English affectations) were the entire top floor of an old warehouse, south of Market Street, in the industrial area of San Francisco. They deserve an extended description.

There was, in reality, one huge room with a ridiculously small stove in the middle which of course didn't heat the place at all adequately. My bed reposed away in one corner, behind a black laquered Japanese folding screen I had found in an antique shop. This bed was always heaped high with quilts and comforters, for the corner was inevitably draughty and damply cold. But it was the quietest, least illuminated spot in the place.

A strange feature of my rooms was a large, peaked skylight, of great height, in the exact middle of the ceiling, over the stove area. To me, it was near useless and even a nuisance on a particularly sunny day, when it tended to act as a gigantic magnifying glass which would shrivel anything placed under it for very long, including people. If it rained, on the other hand, this skylight became a sort of large musical instrument, which always had a soothing, soporific effect on me. At such times, it was very pleasant to sit directly under it and watch the wild coursings of the rainwater, giving oneself up to fantasies and dreams. As an ardent Holmesian, I would often imagine myself in Victorian London, which would always lead me to make a pot of tea and get out biscuits. After this, I would ensconce myself in my large leather chair — which I hauled up the spidery fire escape one night with Seamus' grunting, cursing assistance. (We had rescued this chair from a dusty debris bin — a Dempsey Dumpster, they're known as — as we rambled through the city under the spell of what Seamus called 'Dumpster madness'.) Once I was in this chair, I imagined myself to be in London. And this was not difficult for me, since I once lived there for nearly three years, in a basement flat in Longridge Road, Earl's Court, an area known to locals as 'Kangaroo Valley', due to the large influx of Australians.

From this chair I could also, opening my eyes, look out one of the thirty-two small, longish shaped windows which ringed the enormous room, and see a sight that all who saw agreed was nothing short of marvelous. This was the huge, illuminated glass of beer atop the brewery near-by, which drained and refilled itself once every 36 seconds, and was said to have caused many accidents on the freeway that circled past it. A person with an active mind can readily imagine how entertaining and comforting this landmark was to watch. It was always there and never burnt out nor stopped its draining and refilling, which became strangely reassuring to one after living there awhile.

For me, the sight gained another subtle dimension due to the fact that I disliked beer. I could never see what all the fuss was really about; it's a weak and watery beverage. Of course, it doesn't have to be; I can recall reading about beer and ale in England in the halcyon days before World War I, when it was possible for a traveller in the British Isles to get over 100 different types of domestic beers and ales on the market. Seamus went into pyrotechnics of ecstasy, so to speak, when I told him that fact, for he loved beer. One of his favorite entertainments when he visited me was to smoke hashish and contemplate the immense spectacle of the draining, re-filling glass. He said it assumed cosmic proportions and once he seemed on the point of suffocation in a laughing fit that seized him while we were both absorbed in its grandeurs. Once, during the day, we saw a small figure emerge at the bottom of the glass, and we got out my field glasses to see what was up. It turned out to be what was probably a maintenance man, who clambered up and over the side of the glass, tending to its needs. Seamus compared it, on this occasion, to Mt. Rushmore; 'The Rushmore of Advertising!' he said. I pointed out to him the inaccuracy of this comparison, but he shushed me with the comment that I was too literal minded and that this would lead to all sorts of grief in my life. In fact, this led to one of his numerous harangues against the bourgeoisie, whom he denounced as having the imagination of china cabinets and lace dollies.

Another feature of my quarters that was extremely pleasant was the proximity of a large, commercial bakery. This caused the entire area to often be redolent with the tantilizing smells of fresh baked bread and, no doubt, other savoury pastry delights. To my great good fortune, I succeeded in becoming friends with a night shift employee at this bakery, who gave me immense quantities of baked goods, which was very helpful, due to the wild and erratic fluctuations in my personal finances. Seamus told me I was gorging myself on chemical pastes, but I noticed that he was never a laggard in eating the goods my friend provided.

Along the far wall of my large room, across from the entrance door, was a very large sink, of the industrial type, and my refrigerator, which many people thought, seriously, was one of the first models. I had arranged a small nook, with throw cushions, an Oriental rug I found in an antique stall at a street fair, a small Victorian green divan and my stereo system with records, diagonally across from the sink area. Seamus had suggested that I erect a 'Persian tent' over the huge sink, but I never did this.

My library, which was already large, took up most of the back wall and flowed around the one corner of the room to the door, the shelving running from the floor to halfway up to the ceiling, which was a uniform twenty feet high, except for the towering shaft of the skylight, which I never bothered to measure — although we did once mount an industrial painter's ladder, open a hatch-window of it, and fly a huge Chinese fish kite out of it, to amuse some friends. (This was seen by a television news team, and footage of the kite appeared that evening on the news.) I was very proud of my library. It cost me quite a bit, in the sense that I had to have all the shelves fitted with glass doors, since I discovered that I had developed an allergy to the sort of unique dust that apparently collects only on books. These glass doors could render bizarre visual effects in that large corner of the room, which sometimes startled newcomers. A friend finally generously gave me some draperies, which I hung over the shelves. I could open these like curtains; they served the triple function of decoration, protection of the books from the sun, and added sound muffling, which made that part of the loft almost like another suite of rooms, different from the rest of the place. I would have had my bed there, and often fantasized of laying there amongst my tomes, like a pasha, except that the sight of a bed in that area somehow did not 'fit'.

The water closet (I had a sign lettered W.C., in blue, with a hand pointing, over the appropriate spot; another British eccentricity of mine) was the only part of my apartments that was not on the same floor. And this was often cause for mirth, especially with drunks. The W.C. was reached by descending a steep flight of wooden stairs, down to the ground floor, where the owner of the building had installed a small shower stall and loo. These stairs were covered with a trap door, which posed a considerable hazard when left gaping open by someone who had gone below. I had the stairs railed, but it really was miraculous that no one ever fell headlong into this hole, including myself. This was the only feature of my quarters that I strongly disliked and fretted about. To go down there in the dead of night was harrowing, as it was to go there to shower early, upon just getting out of bed. I finally bought a nightjar, in an 'Americana' shop, and kept this under my bed; no one knew this, though, but me. I also got up a device to entertain guests who had to use the facility and thus endure the rigors of getting to and from it safely. On the wall directly behind

the commode, I hung a doctor's stethoscope, which a
medical friend gave to me. I furnished no instructions on its
use, and none were needed. How often those remaining
upstairs would be regaled by bursts, squeaks, titters, and
roars of laughter from the W.C. below, where the occupant
had obviously found a use for this instrument! It was
delightful. A Shakespearian moment occurred in this
cellarage, one that I love to narrate at parties. An old friend
of mine, who had gone on to become, of all things, an
instructor in sword and combat choreography for a
repertory theater group, was spending the week-end in the
loft. I happened to be in the area and decided that I wanted
a book that was there. I let myself in a downstairs entrance
that I had a key for, but rarely used. I started up the stairs to
the trapdoor, when I detected the obvious sounds of an
amourous struggle above. My friend was protesting his
abiding, deep love to a lady. In his passion, he began to say
vehemently, over and over, that he 'swore' he loved no one
else. I edged up the stairs, until my head was directly under
the trapdoor. As he cited, once again, his faithfulness, his
true deep feelings, I uttered a hoarse, whispering basso cry,
like the Ghost in *Hamlet:*

'Swear!'

My friend chased me for two blocks and the woman left
the place.

Recollecting that event, it strikes me that there were
probably an inordinate number of women who slept with
other men in my rooms. There was something about the
place — perhaps its vastness, its expansiveness — that
seemed to render women giddy and vulnerable to
peccadilloes, once they were in there. One woman
preserved her virtue — a quaint phrase these days, I
suppose — but would climb the fire escape ladder several
times a month to confess her life's ills to me. She would
sprawl on the floor, revealing nearly all, and sometimes
indeed, all there was to reveal, while I sat ensconced in the
antique leather chair, nodding in an imitation of sagacity, at
her outpourings. Everytime she did this she would at some

point remind me that I looked exactly like a priest —
sometimes she said a monk — and then smile broadly, or
even laugh. Seamus said that she was obviously deeply
perverted, and urged me on to 'despoil' her (he loved
archaic words nearly as much as I do). But he was, and is,
prone to very rash actions. I remained, nodding in the chair,
sometimes smoking a long Danish reading pipe a friend
brought back from a year's tour of duty in the US Air Force
at Thule, Greenland. Once I did lay on the floor next to her,
and she abruptly kissed me on the mouth, and said,

'Do you think it's sinful?'

Then she urged me to go out and get her a carton of
chocolate milk, which she was suddenly ravenous for. She
remained the night that time, and I awoke, to see her small
breast exposed, from her stylish green Army fatigue shirt,
there beside me on the floor where we both had fallen
asleep. I was not seized with lust, but rather a feeling of
incredible oafishness and clumsiness. I covered her with a
quilt, and sat reading Robert Burton's *Anatomy of
Melancholy,* watching the beer glass occasionally, until she
woke. The truth was, I liked nice girls, as they're called.

Seamus took to painting or drawing nudes in my rooms,
with the stereo blasting hard rock, as it was then called.
Often what he actually painted was not the nude, however,
but anything else. Once it was 'The Idea of A Beer Glass,
Inspired By Nudity'. I think that was the title. There was no
beer glass, or nude, in this work. His friend, Rob Bergstrom,
then hit on an idea — driving his sportscar on the inter-
urban freeways, Seamus togged out in a WWI leather
aviator's helmet, with straps, flying goggles, and a long
cerise scarf. It was said that his first couple of appearances
on the freeway dressed thusly caused several near-accidents.
The negative print of this photograph, held by a rubber
band, over a loudly ticking clock that had six sets of hands,
set inside a huge gilt 19th century frame, was the final
'piece'. (Seamus nearly always refers to his works as either
'pieces', or 'numbers'. In some way, it seems to me that the
'numbers' are lighter, less serious, than the 'pieces'. I once

asked him about this; he said he had no idea.)

But, as a matter of fact, the WWI flying helmet piece may have been the progenesis of Seamus' intensification of his pioneering art works. He told me that he had learned from a book he saw in a store, while shopping for a gift, that the art object had been de-materialized, and that he, Seamus, had for at least five or six years been what was now called a Conceptual artist. He had decided to devote his entire energies to this, he told me. And a veritable flood poured forth, thereafter. Seamus got into his old MG every day, for a month solid, and had Bergstrom photograph him at various points in and around the city. However, lest the unwary think that he was just a fool, Seamus had Bergstrom take each photograph, or each successive photograph, one minute later than the previous day, *numerically,* not sequentially, and he documented this with a numerical notation on each picture. But, as far as I am aware, only one of these pictures ever actually became a piece, the one I have just previously described. There were immense numbers of stories, however, that something incredible had been done, or was being done — a *performance* piece, it was called, *post-minimalist* style — with these photographs. This pleased Seamus no end, and when I told him that I could probably write a book about the numerous rumors I'd heard about the WWI racing photographs, he laughed and suggested that I do so. I was taken aback.

I can remember many events from this period. Once my landlord came to the loft and witnessed one of Seamus' 'performances' — although by now Seamus and his cognoscenti friends called it 'non-static art'. Seamus did a dance of some sort (he called them 'ritualistic movements, designed to invoke the myth in all of us') in the nude, except for a strange woven band of some sort of fabric and feathers, passed tightly around his chest. The audience, many of whom I didn't know and never did meet, was in darkness, as the whole loft was, except for the intermittent garish strobic beams of a slide projector, which threw photographs over Seamus' cavortings. He leapt, grovelled on the floor, pirouetted, strode in silent movie fashion, as if on a treadmill, and raised his arms in supplicatory fashion. Quite slowly, he took blood from his arm with a hypodermic, and injected it into a large grapefruit, which he then tore open with his hands and ate. (A man threw up in my sink during this part, I later discovered, but he was so discreetly quiet about it that I don't believe anyone heard him.) A tape of Japanese koto music played during the entire event. Seamus abruptly disappeared (through the trapdoor), leaving the ceremonial sash, or whatever it was, laying on the floor; he'd hurled the grapefruit skin into the audience. Just as abruptly, the koto music stopped, the lights came on, and a four-piece rock band, which had somehow been situated on a small platform behind the screens around my bed area, burst into frenetic sounds. A long table was simultaneously moved forward on one side of the loft, on which were cheeses, scooped melon balls, pineapple spears, potato chips, avocado and bean dips, English biscuits and butter and sliced summer sausage, along with five or six gallon jugs of Red Mountain Burgundy wine. Nearly at the same instant, a dense aroma of marijuana smoke began to waft through the loft. People crushed around the table, others began to gyrate on the floor, and a literal cacophony of sound arose. All had been pre-arranged by Seamus, who now re-entered from the basement, clad in a short, open leather jacket, mauve Italian-style tank top, faded Levis, and Frye boots. I overheard him telling two women, who he told me later were 'art student types', that he had studied mime in Paris with Marcel Marceau. Meanwhile, my landlord, whose mouth was agape, tapped me on the shoulder, and asked,

'Does he get *paid* for doing this? Really?'

So things accelerated. Seamus took to holding long discussions with me, and with anyone else who happened to be in the loft. These discussions assumed an almost obsessional need with me, and I got more and more involved, willy-nilly, with his career, and the art world. Finally one night Seamus intensified my involvement by revealing to me his deepest desire in life. He spent the entire evening leading up to it — it was true, as he said that night, that he was 'hopelessly dramatic' — and this included a long walk in a pouring gale-level rainstorm, which he loved. He claimed he always took advantage of a storm to walk in the rain, and informed me, among other things, that he once had visited the Isle of Skye, off Scotland, where there was a yearly average of over 150 inches of rainfall. I had to admit to being dumbfounded when he told me this, standing there on a streetcorner in the gale; he had to shout above the wind for me to hear. Seamus always had the most incredible sorts of apparent trivia at his fingertips and he would pop out with them at the damnedest times. (On a previous walk, he had suddenly asked me, for no apparent reason, if I knew that it was a medical fact that over 40% of the population of the United States had congenitally deviated septums.) It was after this pneumonical stroll, while we hunched, drinking brandy, near the stove back in the loft, with the rain and wind playing a wild symphony on the skylight, that Seamus told me his great goal was an exhibition at *Ace: Venice*. He added, after I'd taken a large gulp of brandy on hearing this, that of course he was not goal oriented. He added that, as far as he was concerned, an artist had no express commitment to consistency, but rather only to 'a consistency of invention'. Thus was his innermost desire imparted to me, while I stared wondering into a brandy snifter.

What a time this was, this so recent past, now so far away! Seamus said it could only be comprehended through the principles of art and simultaneity. A barber named Gomez planted a bomb in the National Headquarters of the Sierra Club, for indeterminable reasons. An acquaintance of Seamus' labored over his doctoral dissertation in the Humanities which argued that bondage and discipline films were, among other things, a safeguard against fascism and fascist overloading of the society. A small cabal of jokesters phoned a serious and distinguished writer resident in the city, very early in the morning, representing themselves as reporters. They informed him he had won the Nobel Prize and asked for an exclusive interview. When the writer finally asked if this was a joke, they told him it was. I received a deluge of letters from a friend who had been a member of several urban and rural communes; then he had 'gone hermetic' in Vermont, and manufactured candles, which were sold in an original American crafts shop. He was obsessed with moving.

> 'Always, always people escaping to a new way of living; in Oregon, in West Virginia, in Arkansas, in Vermont. Only it's not a new way and there's no escape. It's just flight . . . This is a country, man; the USA is a country where IT is always just around the next bend in the mother-fucking road — *THE PLACE,* your place! Only it's not really there. Probably it never was . . . but all these people believe that, man, and they keep hunting for it, like it's *gotta be there!* And I keep trying to tell them, to ask them at least — What if it isn't *there?* Shit, it's enough to drive a man crazy, I'm telling you.'

That's how a letter from him would go. He was a serious person, everyone said. And a poet I knew, who had published eight books of poems, called me and complained bitterly that he had to write short stories to make a living; he asked me why poets did not get paid for what they did, like everyone else. Another person, a woman, got up a grant for a state-funded research project which would inquire into a frequently observed sociological phenomenon, the cessation of listening to rock music by people at certain points in their lives.

This was the milieu, as the sociologists would term it, in which I moved increasingly and in which Seamus worked and schemed. Anything was possible, and, indeed, often happened. When the Southern Pacific Railroad Company demolished their psuedo-Spanish Baroque mission railroad station at Fourth and Townsend Streets in San Francisco,

Seamus and an Irish friend, named Barrie O'Gorman, held
an official 'Wake'. Seamus read a Manifesto, in which he
cited the close friendship, over the years, of the Irish and the
railroads, and denounced the SP's 'rapacious, uncaring and
thieverous actions uponst the fair body of this trembling
city. A most grievous rape, if ever there was one!' His entire
purpose, he said to me, was to incite a riot (which he said
was a true, unrecognized art form of America), and to have
this riot filmed. Unfortunately, the only thing that occurred
was that an old woman threw a rotten egg at him. But even
this was to bear unexpected fruit in the months to come, for
nothing entered Seamus' sphere that did not, it seemed to
me, at least, later re-emerge, transformed into some
structure, eulogy, phantasm, or ritual action — terms he
used for his 'numbers' and 'pieces' increasingly. One night
in the loft, when I accused him of being a dilettante and a
fool, because he answered my earnest question about what
he *really* wanted to do in life with the reply 'my goal is to
someday get a really good pair of sunglasses', he turned
serious.

'Okay — you want to know why I do what I do — right?
I'll give you a parable, as it were. A true story, about myself.
You could call it "Growing Up Serious In America".
Something like that — like a *disease*, you know? . . . okay.'

'When I was about seventeen, my aunt's husband was
going to retire from the electric company, after thirty years
of service. A good job, as they used to say, by which they
meant a regular paycheck. So my uncle, as I always called
him, had given them over thirty of the best years of his
life . . . what he *really* wanted to do, though, was race
pigeons; he had over six hundred of them and I used to go
out with him when he'd take them on training flights. Only
he could never figure out how to make *that* his life . . . you
have to earn a living, he'd say, grinning at me. You know;
how *does* a person make a living racing pigeons? You try to
figure that out — like I did — you may see where I'm
coming from. Okay . . . so my uncle is *retiring* — what a
lousy concept, eh? Retiring; no longer of use to the

corporation. So he'd get a banquet — a cheap one — and some Vice-President would make a speech and they'd give the man an expensive engraved gold watch, a pin, and a two-dollar cigar. And that would be it! One night I was laying on the sofa, doing nothing. My uncle was at work and my aunt was talking about how neat this retirement was going to be; how they would get to go to the National Pigeon Convention every year, and all. And it just hit me! I jumped up; I made a speech to my aunt, rebelling against that whole idea, that whole life style, there in their house, which my uncle had traded his life for to the company . . . you can imagine the effect on my aunt. She was deeply angered, hurt — scandalized, you could say. And it was the first time I saw that I was an adult, that I *could do it!* For me, it was a very significant act, a realization, a *position.* Okay? You see? . . .'

I did. It was about this time that Seamus got a job with the Electric Wastebasket Company. I never discovered exactly what it was that this company did, or made, and I have to say I spent some time in trying to visualize, or conceptualize (I had learned that term/idea from Seamus) what exactly, or even vaguely, an electric wastebasket would do. I think that he may have designed things for them, or even perhaps done lay-outs and that sort of work. Significantly, it was about this time that he tacked up in my loft a gigantic blown-up poster of two eggs frying on a metal representation of the state of Nevada, and placed over it a large numeral, 1. And this was the first of the Egg Events, which made Seamus famous. Whatever happened at the Electric Wastebasket Company — which, like 'The Red Headed League', familiar to all Sherlockians, may not have even existed in reality — Seamus Vincent produced a series of works which electrified the entire art scene. Everyone remembers these, of course. After the Nevada Gambling Eggs (the poster), Seamus did The Earthquake Egg, in which he and Digit Taylor secreted themselves in the TransAmerica Pyramid Building, and, as the sun rose, placed an egg at the apex of the pyramid tip, for which they had to rig a special harness and employ a steeplejack. While a huge crowd gaped in the street below, and the police swarmed up in the elevators and called through bullhorns, the egg was gently nudged off the apex, to fall into the street below. In a piece made in reference to a famous figure of art in the past decade, Seamus opened a dozen and a half eggs in a gallery, all of which had no yoke. This was entitled 'Yok-o-No!' It got a strange mixture of reviews in the press, which led immediately to the 'Egg-Act-ly' show, held in a cellar in North Beach, to which the press were invited. When they arrived, a large number of constructed eggs were 'hatched', and men dressed in suits and ties stepped forth and began to read, simultaneously, a number of artistic and esthetic credos at the tops of their voices. As the critics turned to leave this, a large rooster at the stair head (obviously a person disguised) let loose a veritable flood of eggs down the stairs which caused the critics to, among other things, slip and fall. I've heard that a law suit is still in litigation from this evening's events. In 'Egg-BART', Seamus rode around the BART subway system with huge colored paper eggs, which would be mysteriously thrust out of the train at random stations, astonishing or frightening commuters. Associates placed eggs of a similar construction at random times in the stations and the waiting areas. This event delighted children, and even some brawls ensued over possession of these eggs. Probably the most famous of these Egg Events was 'The Burden of Egg', which was actually a two-part event. In the first part, Seamus walked up and down Twin Peaks carrying two eggs in his outstretched hands, until he collapsed, the collapse being photographed, as were the positions, the trajectories, the falls, and the landings, of the eggs. In the second part, Seamus, anonymously, fried eggs and served them randomly to people in the streets. While he was doing the latter, he wore a small placard that read:

> 'I had been doing those little fruit pictures, some landscapes; that sort of thing. You know?'

Seamus had another Egg Event planned, and that was to be an 'On The Road Egg' event, in which he would push an egg with his nose across the USA, but this was abandoned on Van Ness Avenue one night. Then Seamus embarked, with announcements in the newspapers and in posters plastered over the city, on his 'The Eulogies of Common Sense'. But no one ever saw these, for he vanished for nearly six months, immediately after the announcements.

What could a person do with such a man? With such a friend? I received phone calls from all manner of people looking for him; I began to receive mail — bills, threats, jibes, encomiums. I began to feel that I was caught up in some inexorable process; even more pressing was the feeling that I did not know very much about this process, but should. While I sat in the loft late one night, pondering these things, and looking every so often over at the mound of bedclothes which concealed the latest woman who had come searching for Seamus, the call came. How appropriate it was! Through a multitude of hissing, and what sounded like large waves swelling and falling, Seamus' voice instructed me that a letter would come the next day, which I should act upon immediately, as it was most important to him. He insisted that I promise him that I would act *immediately,* and despite my pleas to know what was going on, I finally assented, not really understanding why or how, or anything else. What was I to 'act immediately' on? I fell into a fitful sleep wondering, and had incredible dreams. In the morning I found out..

The envelope, which arrived Special Delivery, had in it an airlines ticket voucher, via Alitalia Airlines, to Venice, Italy. There was a one-sentence message from Seamus; at least I assumed it was from him:

> 'Modern living converts fiction into fact. Act immediately; come at once.'

There were the inevitable thoughts — the number of people for whom I'd have to concoct explanations, for instance. But the power was on me, and I arrived in Venice, some 18 hours later, after a two-hour layover in Paris, during which time an American businessman was discovered aboard our plane who had no ticket, or passport, and thus could not even be let out of the airport. Apparently, he had been drunk in San Francisco, and somehow boarded the wrong flight. He was by turns contrite and outraged, a very American combination, I thought. I also began to feel that my journey wasn't the only one that would need explanation. Discovering me to be a fellow countryman, he appealed to me frequently with the expression 'Can you believe this? Can you *believe it?*'

I arrived at Venice itself at night, due to the time differential of some eleven hours from San Francisco. Jet lag had me fast by the throat and as I gazed stupidly around the airport, I felt a tug on my sleeve. A seedy greasy-looking man was bowing, tugging, and saying, in a timorous fashion yet with insistence, my name and looking inquiringly at me, especially my shoes, which I've noticed all Europeans seem to look at first. I nodded and he steered me rapidly out of the airport, and into what I took to be some sort of taxi, where his face floated dimly in the back seat across from me, puffing on a villainous smelling cheroot of some sort. He kept up a rambling, incessant chatter, which gave me absolutely no chance to say anything. It was strange that he seemed in fact to be an American himself, and even spoke with what sounded to me like an eastern accent, New England perhaps. He talked about everything and anything, speaking with great rapidity.

'A good flight, eh? I hope they fed you . . . ha, ha! Yes, well, you know, what gets you about Americans — hey, listen, I include myself, don't worry — what really gets you is their phony neighborliness. Isn't that right? You've thought of it, I'm sure; you look like a very intelligent man. After all —'

'I've never thought of it, to tell you the truth. What I'm wondering now is what I am doing here, really; that's the thing, Mr. — ah —'

'It's a fundamental dishonesty, oh, yes! Yes. This

neighborliness. Because it's all a put-on, isn't it? Really. Because its real purpose is, of course, to see if you're, quote, *normal* . . if you're okay. So it is actually a spy mission, for the collection of community gossip. To get at you, you know; very vicious . . . of course, the city *used* to enrich people, but now —'

'Fundamental dishonesty? You know, I —'

'Actually, what I was thinking of was, that before I got here, I was at one of those points in my life when I thought I knew everything. You know the way that gets?'

'Well —'

'Certainly. And what I was really headed for — listen, I think that I was headed for being the worst thing in the world, maybe. You know? Turning out to be a 45-year old over-suntanned Californian. In faded Levis, with turquoise jewelry! Thinking that I'm doing T'Chi, or something.'

'I thought that —'

'Going out to the beach, late at night, and building a fire. Taking a nude swim, rubbing sand on my leathery hide, and staring intensely out at the ocean, hunkered down there by the fire. Muttering . . . waiting for the dawn, you know. Across from me, with an adoring look on her face, is an 18 year-old high school escapee. A daring, rebellious thing — all that shit out of old surfer movies, and encounter groups. . . You know?'

He laughed loudly.

'If I knew what —'

'The end of the road, brother! Whew! Can you imagine it? Then you start thinking; maybe you could go to Peru . . . someplace like that. Honduras, Costa Rica — one of those banana republics in Central America. I've heard that Costa Rica's pretty good these days.'

'Is that so? But what —'

'We're here — look sharp.'

We had arrived during this monologue in what must have been the city of Venice itself. When I opened the door of the cab, I immediately recognized the smell of the sea and other heavier, ranker odors. We were at a canal, in fact. Peering about me I saw a gondola below, and steps, and heard the lapping sounds of the water. I called out, looking around.

'Seamus? . . .'

The man in the cab gestured to me and waved.

'Well, sport, as they say, it's all yours now. Have a good time, whatever you do, okay?'

I lunged back towards the cab.

'For God's sake, man, don't leave me here like —'

'Arrivederci — it's been fun for me.'

The door slammed; the cab sped off, and I swayed in its exhaust and sprayed gravel, wondering if I was about to faint.

And then it was quite quiet. I turned around several times, looking about me, and called Seamus' name into the dark night. Far off I could hear the occasional hoot of a ship's horn, and the sound of motor launches. That this was Venice, the ancient city on the Adriatic Sea, and that I was in it, swirled in my brain, and I looked for a place to sit down, thinking, strangely, that I should have taken up smoking again, for I badly needed a cigarette. The only thing I could see very clearly, other than the street stretching away behind me and clumps of darkened buildings, was the gondola, the steps leading down to it. In fact, a small light was on in the slightly swaying boat.

I made my way hesitantly down the very wet, slippery steps, with the proverbial thousand thoughts running through my mind. Where was Seamus? What was going on, and why was it happening thusly, and why to me? What might be the purpose of this gondola; who, what might be in it? I stopped several steps above it and called Seamus' name again, but there was still no answer. Silence; only the louder, nearer lapping of the canal waters, which now were close below me. It flashed through my mind, absurdly, that I could be mugged on the spot and dumped into the canal. Stories I had once read of the cruelties of the Doges of Venice — the garrot, the Bridge of Sighs — came to me. And just as abruptly, for whatever unknown reasons of fear, folly, or curiosity, I leapt down the remaining steps, and into the gondola, and yelled, at the top of my voice.

'ALL RIGHT! ALL RIGHT! COME ON!'

The rush of adrenaline left me puffing, almost breathless, and I stared wildly around, nearly falling from the agitated swaying of the gondola. Nothing; only echoes. The feel of being on water suddenly made me nauseous, and I felt I was going to vomit; I lurched towards the light in the far end of the gondola, in what appeared to be a sort of curtained off area. I threw back the heavy curtains and fell on a leather cushion, groaning. And then I saw it.

There, on the small table near the cushions, was a large antique playing card, like a Tarot card, a really outsized one. It was an Ace of Diamonds. At first, thinking that I was hallucinating, I shook my head, and rubbed my eyes. But that's what it was. Can you imagine it! I took it up — I could hold it like a book — and found there was a note pinned to the back of it, written in a beautiful calligraphic style.

> 'The fear of exhibiting "bad taste", of having people "Tch, tch" over your choices, your pleasures, your enthusiasms, is a very unfortunate one.'

I fell back among the leather cushions; literally a million conflicting feelings and impressions were running through me. And then the curtains parted and there was Seamus, grinning at me. I felt a wild surge of anger, and struggled to rise, but fell among the cushions. Seamus had a bottle of Strega in one hand and he made a gesture through the curtain with the other, obviously to a gondolier, for before I could move again, we were out on the water, and a glass of Strega was in my one hand, and a cigarette in the other. Seamus lit it. He sat down across from me then, and said

'Venice is the most magic city in the world, perhaps. You know that?'

'Jesus, Seamus! For Christ's sake!'

I said something else, incoherently, I think. He continued to smile at me, and waved his hand slightly towards my glass.

'Have some of that. It's good stuff. You and me are going to see this city. You know, they say that industrial pollution's going to rot the place away — literally eat it *up!* — in about thirty more years. So we'll see it . . . Now, tell me about your flight.'

We spent four days in Venice, and then Seamus returned with me to San Francisco. On the flight back, he disclosed to me that he had a show that was to open very shortly at *Ace: Venice* Gallery, in Los Angeles. He had 'made' it in L.A. He always liked to say 'L.A.', saying it with a peculiar relish, usually grinning raffishly, and leaning confidentially towards you, saying 'L.A., man! *L.A.!'*

The show was a stunner, he said; it would be called 'The Process of Process; or, The Performance of Performance', and it consisted in the gallery itself being locked and blacked out — windows, doors, everything — for two weeks. No one would get in. That was it. He laughed, I remember, and leaned forward to me, in a conspiratorial manner, and said

'L.A., man! L.A.! The city of the future! *The* heavy art mart, right? Holy shit! And they'll come, and they'll wonder, and wonder, and wonder. WONDER! Huh?'

He punched and dug me in the ribs, and I could feel my eyes were big behind my glasses. Some people in the plane were looking around. I nodded.

'But they won't even get into the bloody fucking gallery! Ohh, Jesus! Jesus! Mama Mia!'

He threw his head back, stamped his feet, and gave out with a terrific sort of braying laughter that he had when really worked up, that was impossible to ignore, or know what to do with. I grinned weakly at some of the people who now stared openly.

'Seamus, do you really think that —'

He cut me off, suddenly stopped laughing.

'No! No, it'll be a really great piece. A fine work. You wait and see. I'm surprised no one's thought of it before . . . it's so fucking apparent, isn't it? I love it, I *love* it!'

When we got back to the loft in Enterprise Street, fresh

from the airport, I asked Seamus again about what had gone on in Venice, in connection with me. The flight, the gondola, all of it. He had refused to talk of it there, saying it would spoil everything.

'That's the art of the future, what you were *in*. That's it. And you still can't believe it, right? . . . I mean, *that* was personal art, with real meaning, no? It was just for you. Pure autobiography, okay? And it was a great piece, too. Don't you agree, really?'

'Seamus . . . I really feel confused, to tell you the truth.'

He beamed at me, and grasped my arm.

'Good! That's good! I couldn't ask for more, and neither could you.'

'But — I mean — I just can't really believe it — the whole thing — why? I mean, *why?* What's going on, that this —'

'It's not documented, either', he said winking at me. 'Done only one time.'

We were standing near the long windows of the loft, and we could see that beer glass out there on the brewery — the icon of modern living, as Seamus once called it — filling and re-filling, just as always. And we just stood there; we fell silent, and just watched that damn thing, that neon glass, staring. The glow of it filled the room and winked and flashed. I don't know how long we stood there like that, except that I know I became intensely conscious of us both standing there, in that glow, looking. Finally, Seamus touched me on the arm, and said he wanted to tell me about his next work which he said would be a large, public piece. He gesticulated wildly with his hands, shaping in the air.

'It's gonna be about freeways, see? The freeways? Nobody's done anything, *really,* with them — except myself, that thing about seven years or so ago — with that photo-journalist — what was his name? That guy, you know —'

'Rob Bergstrom.'

'Right! The very man! You gotta helluva memory, you know that?'

'The freeways —' I interjected. I was eager to hear him.

'Oh, yeah! I'm gonna call it — let's see . . . 'How to Starve
On 100 Miles a Day; or, Why Be An Expatriate?' And I'll
just be laying around, just getting that California
unemployment tan, you know? It's the California secret,
see?'

We laughed a big back-slapping laugh, both our heads
thrown back.

We started then to talk. We talked about the freeways,
and the German Autobahns and the old Italian road race,
the Mille Miglia, which Seamus said was a great art form,
especially when Stirling Moss drove in it. At four thirty a.m.
he left, clambering down the metal frame fire escape,
waving as he walked out to the main street. On an impulse, I
went immediately to my bookcase, and read Gary Synder's
'North Beach Alba'. I put my hand right on it. The sun came
up, and it was making one of those travel poster dawns,
those gorgeous California golden dawns, over San
Francisco, which looked so clean and sparkling in the new
light. I decided that I'd get out up on the roof that very day,
and start getting a tan myself; it was definitely, as Seamus
had said, a good idea, a good project. And the next week the
show at *Ace: Venice* did open. But I'm not going to tell you
about that. You wouldn't believe it.

TOULOUSE-LAUTREC

I first met him in an English-style bar — one of those places that tries to look like a real pub; they have an elaborate electric fire contraption inside a cute fireplace, with a couple of commercially manufactured oak beams above it. Maybe a few copper kettles and such hung about. They hire a barmaid who says she's from Manchester, or Leeds; a stringy red-head, or a busty, floozy blonde, although once in a while they luck out and get the real thing; a woman who is milk-maid fresh, whom the grit of the place doesn't seem to touch. Usually brunettes, these, with large, astonishing eyes, extremely clear, and dazzling white teeth. You get an idea of what England was two hundred years ago when you see her.

But this isn't a story about England, or barmaids, so I'd best get on with it, then. At that time I used to be an habitue of this pub. I was unknown then, a struggling writer with every foible and debility that such an identity implies. I would sit in the pub — which was subtly called Ye Bull n' Bush — dreaming of my future literary triumphs. I was as yet not involved in the work that would underlie that fame, of course. As with many young writers, I had easily, at my fingertips, you may say, the excuse — if, indeed, any were needed — for my hours of apparent idleness there in the pub. I was gathering material for my writing.

Of course, the underlying reality of my own deception was that I was, indeed, gathering material. But, at that time, I now suspect that I sat there to gather women, if any were available. Failing that, I hoped, obscurely, to meet either a kindred soul, preferably literary, but with less talent than me, or some editor or publisher, who would solicit a manuscript from me, which he (or, even better, a young

lovely she) would call me about three days later, in rapt
voice informing me of imminent publication, a large cash
advance on my royalties, a very active PR campaign in the
major media and the forwarding to me of a set of plane
tickets to Guadalajara, or Mazatlan, where a first-class hotel
awaited me, and a month's paid vacation.

It was obvious that I had little experience with editors
and publishers. In fact, I had none, for in those days I
believed a living in literature was an easy matter and almost
automatically lucrative. As an evening would wear on, and I
drank more of the dark Mackeson Stout that was my
especial favorite, I would become more assured of the ease
and relative accessibility of literary and financial success.
That the two might not be yoked rarely bothered me,
although I had heard, of course, the usual stories from my
cronies. There was X, reputed to be the finest lyric poet of
his generation, and a derelict, a wino. There was A, who'd
published nine books and was forced to work at a
succession of mediocre, menial jobs to pay his bills. There
was Z, who lived on Public Assistance. Y had become a
photo-journalist. And H was supported by his wealthy
uncle from Minnesota.

However, I took little notice of this cavilling. After all,
many of my writer friends were quite apparently riddled
with that savage disease of most writers: envy. One of the
prime topics of conversation whenever we were together
was invariably the utter worthlessness of the latest
publications and, more especially, the hacks who sold out
and published their drivel and tripe in their glossy pages,
next to advertisements for prophylactics, whiskey, athletic
supporters, hairpieces and stereo equipment. Those who
received the worst pilloring were writers who won prizes.
It was held as a truism in these diatribes that the very fact of
a writer winning the Nobel Prize, for instance, meant that
said writer was 'over the hill', and finished. And, in any case,
why did such writers insist on publishing in magazines,
when they didn't need the money and could get anything
they wrote published anytime, anywhere? It kept down the

younger writers, who thus could *never* get published. The
only authors who could escape this contumely were those
who were dead. The fact of a writer being dead changed all,
and some dead writers were, admittedly, good — even great
— writers. They deserved to be published, no doubt of it.

Such was the nature of our discourse in our meetings at
the pub, or at some other drinking establishment. The
affinity of literary men for alcohol is a long-established
verity. We rarely met in restaurants, primarily because,
when it comes down to it, most writers perfer drink to food,
if their funds are meagre. Drink is inspiring, or at least
results in a few hours of comfortable oblivion, whereas
food, although physically necessary, is in the same category
as sleep, a banal biological necessity to be got through as
quickly as possible.

Ye Bull n' Bush was a spot where one could hope to meet
another writer, or even a poet, although the latter had a
curious habit of keeping to themselves, like musicians, or
ballet dancers. Also, one could avoid other writers with
some degree of safety in Ye Bull because a tradition of
courtesy prevailed there, which permitted one to ignore
another writer, merely by turning away, not making eye
contact, stuffing one's head studiously behind a book or
paper, or replying in unintelligible monosyllables, such as
'Ummm' and 'Uhh', to solicitous inquiries and 'openers'.
There was one writer, by the name of Harrington, however,
who did not observe the etiquette of Ye Bull. Harrington
was among the more peculiar of our set, if such a distinction
really has any meaning, in that he had become obsessed with
the covers of books of matches, among other equally odd
obsessions — although perhaps not actually odd in a person
devoted to words, to the language. Harrington was known
as an experimental writer. It was said that he had, for some
months, been at work on a new story that revolved around
the slogans on matchbooks.

Harrington would seize upon people in the pub without
regard for any of the traditions of privacy, tact or snobbery.
The seizure would be accelerated if an individual happened

to pull out a book of matches with a slogan written on it.
Harrington was there like a cat pouncing.

'Become A Television Technician', he would crow,
holding up the pack. 'Oh, Jasus, that's a rich one!'

Among Harrington's personal favorites — he revealed
this to me a number of times — were those covers exhorting
one to seize the vast economic opportunities to be had by
learning various subjects at home — such as Law, Account-
ing, Refrigeration Engineering, Motel Management, Auto
Mechanics, and Philately — in a remarkably short period of
time, while continuing to hold down a full-time job.

Such were Harrington's pursuits and he was allowed his
idiosyncrasy. One woman friend who had been in his
apartment told of boxes of matchbook covers laying about,
amid other debris, a major part of which seemed to consist
of bumper stickers, advertising placards, tin can labels, and
newspaper advertisements, all of which she said Harrington
utilized in his writings. Harrington's best friend, who to my
knowledge never came into Ye Bull, was a certain L.J.T.
Reed, who had published 137 selections, from seven
unpublished novels, in various magazines, and was a high
school teacher. Although Reed never came to the pub — he
was reported to be one of those writers with great discipline,
who worked an invariable five hours a night, letting
absolutely nothing interrupt him — his exploits of
publication naturally amazed and intrigued all of us. After
all, how can a writer publish such a bulk of material, and yet
remain obscure, even unknown? After one of Reed's
fragments was read out loud to us at the pub one evening, I
was less doubtful about the answer to this perplexing
question, but it still remained a thorn in the side of many
young writers there. The denunciations, imprecations,
hurled insults, oaths and curses would have made a book in
themselves; indeed, I considered trying to tape several
evenings' worth, which would have been all that I needed,
but I was certain I would be detected.

One writer, who had come in second in a national fiction
contest two years in a row, liked to sit in a large chair in front

of the fireplace, drinking pernod and damning the whole of Academia for the current state of affairs in fiction. He always ended his harangues with the implication that he would soon move abroad (by which he meant Western Europe) where things were better for writers. In fact, he was so vehement about moving that the rest of us were very surprised to find him back, in front of the fireplace, drinking pernod, every week.

A small group of writers there at Ye Bull — four or five of them, at most — liked to argue that the days of intelligent writing were over and that the serious writer was the publisher's only reason for existence. They demeaned the seeking of profit and independent means through writing, held all artists should teach or do manual labor (preferably the latter) to earn their living, and endlessly debated as to what were the true distinctions between fiction and non-fiction.

Then there was the writer who always clamored for writing 'out of the streets'. That was his phrase. He said he was sick of the effusions of over-sensitive and over-civilized white pansies, and that it was time 'to hear from the people'. He was a poor dialectician, but he growled very well. Although he could not give a clear indication of what the vox populi was, or what it would write, or wanted to hear, he knocked another writer through the pub doors one evening, in response to a query as to how one could really be 'over-civilized'.

Certainly it was a lively circle there at Ye Bull n' Bush, and I sometimes wondered if we would go down in literary history. After all, similar very small writers' groups had changed the course of literature, and become world-famous. There had been The University Wits, The Kit-Cat Club, The Literary Club, The Lake School, The Symbolists, The Spasmodics, The Parnassians, and The Expatriates, to name but a few. What would we be called? The invention of an appropriate literary history for us became a theme I still toy with, suitable perhaps even for a short novel.

We had the appropriate setting to become a famous literary group, for we were all living in San Francisco. 'The City', as it is referred to by cognoscenti and aficionados, probably possesses more literary aspirants and pretenders than even the London of olden times (before television) and is, of course, perhaps one-thirtieth the size of that great literary capital of England, and the world. In this Baghdad-by-the-Bay, as San Francisco is also sometimes called, a new novel, poem, story, vignette, play, or sequence is probably being devised nearly every second. Writers prowl through North Beach, slouching in their Navy peajackets in the fogs of July, cigarettes glowing. Coit Tower looms in a strange, shrine-like flood-lit illumination, over Telegraph Hill, where the successful, rich writers live. By day, the unreal-looking Golden Gate Bridge gleams red in the Pacific sunlight, connecting San Francisco to the rest of America, but only tenuously. Literary history, in the shapes of Jack London, Frank Norris, Gertrude Stein and The Beat Generation, is kept alive in coffeehouse conversations, along with the endless betting on who, of the living writers of San Francisco, will become a giant, a myth. In this atmosphere, one nearly has to be a writer; at least it was easier to feel that one was, than in, say, Meridian, Kansas, or some such place. And often 'The City' itself was the topic of discussion — it was too easy to live there, a number of writers complained; you could get nothing done, for daily life was too gentle, with the California sun giving you clear, crystal days, with all the temptations of pleasure for which San Francisco is famous, at your feet. New York writers especially harped on this theme. The City was too sweet, too soft, and kept a man from his work.

Toulouse-Lautrec first came into Ye Bull n' Bush during an argument on this subject of living in The City and what it did to you. I don't think too many people noticed him; he sat with his beer, on the outside of the circle around the fireplace. Two young secretaries were sitting between him and me; they were wide-eyed with eagerness and kept whispering snatches of audible conversation about 'some of them are famous' and 'brilliant poets', while crossing and recrossing their legs, dangling their stylish shoes on their toes. None of this was being neglected by the pernod-drinking denouncer of academic writing and would-be expatriate, who held forth in stentorian tones about how it was useless to work, anyway, since you couldn't get published unless you knew someone. He knew at least twelve different writers of excellence — an even dozen, he emphasized — who could not find a publisher for their works, after years of effort.

'Better to be an opium addict,' he said, raising his hands, palms up. 'That's the thing to do, really. Go to Tangier, or Morocco, or Tunisia and cultivate your dreams. They'll let you in peace there.'

Toulouse-Lautrec laughed, and called over to me:

'What's the point of that, eh?'

So we met. He learned over the two secretaries and introduced himself, adding that, to him, the thing was 'to get on with the job of writing; to *do* it!' The young secretaries smiled hesitantly and left soon after. It was thus that the pernod-drinker — his name was Vladimir Mondini — also met Toulouse-Lautrec, for he came back to me to ask where the two women who'd been sitting there had gone. He did not seem to care for the new member of our set, however, and asked me how it was that I could let 'two lambs like those two' slip through my fingers, ending up by saying, to the room in general, that the drinking of absinthe should be revived and that we could see the accurate portrait of American womanhood by looking at that woman pictured on the Yuban coffee cans. Lautrec laughed, and told me that Mondini showed some imaginative abilities.

Several things about this man Lautrec came out quickly. The first was that no one could ascertain if he was in any way related to the famous French painter. It was noted that Henri de Toulouse-Lautrec had died in 1901, the last male of his line, with no known heirs. The man who entered Ye Bull n' Bush that night was not dwarfish in size and never revealed why his name was what it was. After some

considerable thought on the matter, I came to the conclusion that he could as well have that name as any other —
say, Vladimir Mondini, for instance. No one doubted that
that was Mondini's real name and no one thought it an odd
name. As a matter of fact, it was a good name for a writer, as
many of us often commented. It had a literary sound to it, a
ring.

However, since Toulouse-Lautrec introduced himself by
that name, and never gave any first name, there was
continual agitation about him. A number of people said that
it was obvious what he was doing. He was going around
with a pseudonym. He had had the audacity to pick a really
well-known one, too. This was offered as a conclusive proof
of his stupidity and superficiality, for who, with *any* degree
of imagination, would use a pseudonym such as Toulouse-
Lautrec? Several of my closest friends thought he was
probably a mild psychopath of the harmless variety, with
megalomaniac, paranoid tendencies. Others thought he was
just plainly a bull-shitter and a phony, a poseur of a type to
be found in any literary circle. Whatever he was or was not,
he made an indelible impression on all of us; no one would
argue about that, I'm certain.

He appeared at Ye Bull over a period of about two
months. I don't actually recall how many times he was there;
it was not every night, but it was not extremely infrequently,
either. He seemed to particularly like me, and would catch
my eye if I entered and he was already there, almost
immediately. There was, to me, a strange prescient quality
about him. Even stranger was the immediate knowledge
that spread through the room as soon as he entered, that he
was there. I would feel an irresistible urge to turn around;
there he would be, perhaps ordering at the bar, smiling at
me. I became known as his friend, although such was not
really the case.

He usually sat in the outer ring of chairs round the
fireplace at Ye Bull, and he would speak very little. He
rarely entered into a full-fledged conversation — except
with me — and never into an argument. I think the latter

never occurred for the simple reason that nearly all of us were afraid of him, although it would have been hard to say precisely why we were. He was not authoritarian when he did speak; usually, it would be in the way of a comment on a remark by someone else. Often, when he said these things, he'd wink at me, and I found this utterly disarming and disconcerting. That wink!

Rumors were beginning to spread about him and they were getting numerous by the night I want to talk about. Nobody could find out exactly where he lived; nobody could remember him from anywhere else — say, Berkeley, or Santa Cruz, or even Los Angeles. Nobody knew exactly what it was he did for money, for a living, as it's called. He said that he was a writer, pure and simple, and was 'just knocking about a bit'. No one believed that, though. How could somebody 'just knock about', as he put it? And why did he use that phony English idiom, anyway?

I recall very well that night it finally happened. A very thick fog settled in over the city, and I felt like Sherlock Holmes as I walked towards Ye Bull n' Bush. In fact, I had been enjoying the fog so much, seeing it swirling and eddying outside my apartment windows earlier in the evening, that I'd gotten down my volume of Conan Doyle and re-read several stories, relishing them hugely.

A tumultuous discussion was on that night, mainly between Harrington and Mondini. Harrington had actually sold a story. It's easy to imagine the effect this had on our coterie. No one there had published much at all; Mondini had had a couple of 'vignettes' printed, in those 8½ by 11 mimeographed magazines. A couple of poets there had published rather widely, but no one took them very seriously, and, anyway, everyone knows that poets don't get paid for their poems, so they were pretty irrelevant. But Harrington had *sold* his story to a very highly thought-of journal, called *Ramifications*. This was big-time stuff and Harrington had received a healthy check for his work. Toasts, envy and controversy went forward there that evening, nearly, as the cliché has it, hand in hand.

Toulouse-Lautrec entered in the midst of a foray over a national contest that was going to award a large cash prize and a grant to the writer of a volume of short stories, or 'short fiction', as they termed it. The argument centered around how one should finish a story, or wind up a collection of them, and the immense problems ending things presented in writing. Harrington and Mondini were vehement in their contentions; the statements and theories of Poe, Chekhov, Henry James, Vladimir Nabokov, Edmund Wilson, Ernest Hemingway, Maupassant, and Percy Lubbock flew through the air.

Toulouse-Lautrec, as I say, entered right into the middle of this dispute, and it was truly a dramatic entrance. For one of those strange, impenetrable reasons of timing, a quiet lull in the controversial storm occurred just as he entered the doors. He was wearing his cape that night; this was a British cavalry officer's cape, or cloke, that chained at the throat with silver links, and was nearly full-length. Lautrec had a sort of stylish, rakishly cut black dress hat on that looked rather like a cut-down black Stetson hat and a mauve scarf that flowed over his shoulder; he carried a silver-headed cane that I had never seen him with before, and wore grey gloves, which he peeled off slowly, standing in the doorway. A large whisp of fog had swirled in around him as he entered. The doors banged shut loudly behind him, and everyone looked.

'Jesus! Look at that!' Mondini said, gaping. 'It's Toulouse-Lautrec.'

It was certainly amazing, that entrance. Lautrec bowed slightly to all of us, and went to the bar. The argument heated up again, although some of the people were obviously still intrigued by Toulouse-Lautrec. He came and joined the circle, sitting down next to me, and winked.

The arguments about how to write raged on for at least another hour there by the fireplace. At one point, a poet by the name of Palladin swayed to his feet, and began to read an obscene poem, in heroic couplets, which he prefaced with a dedication to the two daughters of the owner of Ye

Bull n' Bush, a Scotsman named Ian. Ian, perhaps drunker than the poet, came flailing like a windmill off his barstool at the bar's end, but fell ignominiously facedown onto the floor before he reached Palladin. This momentary diversion was ended by the attempted ejection of Palladin and a defense of literary freedom by his fellow writers, which resulted in his being permitted to stay, if he would not read any more that night. Toulouse-Lautrec made very little comment during any of these arguments, although he called my attention to Palladin's use of heroic couplets in his poem. It was strange to observe that the disputants, mainly Harrington and Mondini, continually glanced in Lautrec's direction, as if seeking confirmation of what they were saying.

The argument had reverted to how one should end a story or a piece. What was the *perfect* ending, and how was it achieved? Why did it give satisfaction? Was it, in fact, even attainable; did not the basic laws of physics show us that nothing ever actually ended? What was perfect, and what was an ending, in any case? The question and answers and new questions flew thick and fast, and even the patrons at the bar, who usually were devoted to the exclusive discussion of sex, sports and the weather, not necessarily always in that order, were all turned toward the fireplace, listening.

I made off to the bathroom, finally, having imbibed freely all evening. When I returned, a very heated exchange had sprung up between Mondini, Harrington, and one of the group of writers who liked to argue incessantly over what was fiction and what was non-fiction. Suddenly Toulouse-Lautrec was on his feet. He smiled, looking around the room; he was, I noticed, already lifting his scarf and hat from his chair. An absolute silence fell over the pub, and, for some seconds, only the sound of the fire crackling in the fireplace could be heard. I remember thinking what a soothing, good sound it was.

Mondini signalled to Lautrec, asking him if he had anything he wanted to say. Everyone was leaning forward, very expectantly; even the two bartenders had stopped drying glasses and were standing, leaning forward onto the bar, looking at Lautrec. Then he spoke.

'I've been listening to you all and this is what I would like to say to you. You ask about the perfect story, the perfect ending, the perfect climax.'

He looked around the room, and began to put on his cape.

'Well, my friends —'

There was a sniggering sound, but it was abruptly cut off. Lautrec continued.

'Yes . . . thank you. To go on, then, with what I would like to say. The perfect story, the perfect *ending* of a story, is like the perfect Muse-woman.'

The sniggering sound began again, then quickly ceased. Lautrec looked around the room, then put on his cape, linked the silver chain, and began to pull on his gloves.

'It does not exist. Just as *she* does not exist,' he said then, lifting his stick. He tapped it lightly on a table, as a murmur had broken out when he had spoken the last sentence.

'And that is the lesson of fiction, and of life.'

Well, you can imagine what happened. A perfect hullabaloo broke forth. Several people came forward at Lautrec, but he was already nearly to the door. I rushed after him myself and we all poured out into that dense fog that was swirling up California Street. We stood there, milling around him. He looked at us; there were some slight words; someone in the back of the crowd said, loudly:

'Well, if there's no perfect ending, what the hell *is* there, then, smart guy?'

There were some muttered 'Yeahs!', and head-nodding. Toulouse-Lautrec was already heading out into the street; he turned, gestured around him with his cane, smiled, and said:

'There's only reality, gentlemen. Only reality.'

A loud howl went up from the group. There we stood, in that fog, not really arguing now, but uttering various exclamations and epithets. And he was gone, right into that fog, probably boarding the California Street cable car; we could hear its bell clanging loudly as it passed up the street.

So we were left there, outside the pub, with everyone commenting on what Toulouse-Lautrec had said. After all, as Mondini said, the whole thing was outrageous, incredulous, and absolutely pretentious; his entrance, his pronouncements, his exit. Who the hell was he, anyway? Who did he think he was, too, to say that about a story having no perfect ending, and so on?

Then we filed slowly back into Ye Bull n' Bush and the argument continued long into the night. It was carried over to The Raven, a restaurant on the opposite corner, when the pub closed at 2 am. The thing that really got me about the whole event, though, was that Toulouse-Lautrec never came back there, at least not as far as I know. Where *did* he go, and who was he? People at Ye Bull began making Lone Ranger jokes about him and the incident. The whole business was just unbelievable, when I think of it. Unbelievable.

I myself kept on with my work, wondering about him often, but more and more pressed into my own work; in fact, now I'm gaining a following of sorts — or so they tell me — and writing more and more, and getting it published. Things have taken a turn, as the English say; that's for certain.

And Ye Bull n' Bush is thriving, I understand, too. But, really, when I think of it, it was not very long after this same incident that I ceased being a regular at Ye Bull and, in fact, I hardly go there at all anymore; usually, only if an old friend takes me there. Of course, a number of the old crowd are still there, still arguing. After all is said and done, it is a comfortable place, there's no denying it.

But, as they say, I've moved on.

SUNDAY
AFTERNOON

We were riding, the four of us in the late afternoon in the weak, autumnal sunlight of November. The trees were now nearly bare of leaves, perhaps at their most beautiful before winter. We really had nothing much in mind . . . we came into a village; very small and very quiet. Charles had driven the road before, we knew where we were, but wanted some direction to the river.

The dog got out, we asked around, but not much was offered in the way of concrete information; it was disappointing. We drove on and the little road spun out, curved, dipped, swayed, etched over the hills out in front of us. We had set out a couple of weeks ago on a similar journey, but we could not find any therapists.

There was further down the twisting, interminable road, an island off-shore, seemingly near in the light, hazy fog. The river. It reminded one of Venice; the colorations, tones of light.

We saw a woman in a Fendi jacket on the shore walking back and forth, back and forth. Her hair was honey-colored, full, rich, long like a mane; eyes a gem-like green. Her mouth was full, pouting. The dog spoke to her, but she did not reply. A curious skiff-like boat went by near shore; in it was a man in a hunting jacket with shooting patches. He was wearing Ralph Lauren Polo.

Then the sun came through, a watery, coppery tone, and we could make out some people in Krizia sweaters with lions on them, hats like Tibetan gear, and pants — marching in some sort of procession. One person lagged at the end; this figure held up a startlingly neon-like sign which read
'The Glory of Missoni'
Another woman emerged suddenly, from high swaying

reeds near the shore. She was wearing an Emba Jasmine and Azurene mink coat, opened to reveal that she had on only a bra and panties, with stack-heeled beige pumps.

'I've seen that woman all over,' Lew said. 'You never know where she's liable to turn up.'

Amazingly, there was a bouncy young girl running down the path near the river, hair streaming back like a modern Diana attired all in Courreges. A thoughtful young woman, hands in khaki pants, walked slowly on the path behind her in a rust-colored heavy knit Perry Ellis sweater. She was pensively happy.

We were going pretty slow; a car passed us — a woman we knew, in a very handsome grey Evan-Picone jacket . . . or was it Guy Laroche? This woman worked Sundays because it was quiet then she said, and you could get things done. No interruptions.

There was a woman hitch-hiking. Or maybe just there, by the side of the road wearing a Basile jacket of wool tweed, Napa leather and diamond patterned rabbit. A Buddha-like smile. One foot, in a slim buff boot, gracefully put out. How many women could *stand* like that?

Pete was talking about Heather, who lived on the second floor of his cottage in Red Bluff. 'A Huck Finn town in California,' he said, leaning back in the seat. 'Expect to see a side-wheeler comin' down the Sacramento one a these days. Got up to 121 last summer ya know . . . kinda town where there's white picket fences, fruit trees in your gardens and the people sit on rocking chairs on their porches, just rockin'.'

Heather had gone quail hunting, he said, and was going to teach him how to square dance. She had two shotguns in a case in the hall in the cottage, and disliked men who chewed tabacco; it was too much, she said. She also played the accordion. Pete told us to drive up some Sunday and we'd all get together.

We came up into another village. A woman walked slowly on the bumpy sidewalk. Charles, who didn't talk much, said

'It's her Calvins. I wonder how she got in them.'

'Shoehorn,' Lew muttered.

Even as we looked she met and greeted another woman, who was literally sparkling in Mary McFadden silver pants and pumps. 'Come-fuck-me shoes, those are,' Lew said dryly. Golden Autumn Leaves from Tiffany, graced her slender, arching throat, wonderful against her luminous skin. She had a Cartier watch, with emeralds. An unusual sight, as we passed out of the village, was a large number of wicker hampers stacked in a cul-de-sac.

It was pleasant in the car as evening came on fully. The feel of the Brooks Brothers Oxford button-down shirt, which got increasingly softer as it got older. So did the Shetland sweaters, too. No elbow patches on them though. Simple elegance.

Lew was taking notes again, with his gold pen; he'd go home later and type them up on his Olivetti Praxis 35 electronic typewriter. He looked up, and said he wanted to stop somewhere and get some Neutrogena soap to keep his hands really clean for handling his soft contact lenses. Then he read us a squib, with a tiny pen light he had, from the newspaper. A woman, occupied in the ladies room in a restaurant in town, had suddenly found a live lobster next to her, that proceeded to pinch her boots. She was rescued by the hostess and two waiters, who returned the lobster to its tank.

Behind a screen of slender trees, we saw a woman in a gold Albert Nipon dress walking to her house tucked back in the woods. Little squares of light from its windows were visible through the trees.

We ended up at a place Charles knew, on an inlet on the coast, an English country-style inn. We played darts, backgammon, had some sandwiches and lager, and finished it off by the big baronial walk-in fireplace with glasses of armagnac.

Lew was going to a class in Job Control Language and then, later in the month, one on Information Mapping, a

new business writing technique. He liked the Text Proces-
sing System he was working with, but thought the format-
ting commands were somewhat tricky; what was lasered out
was not always what had been put in. The TSO people were
always worrying about CICS being down, too . . . and it frequently was! Too much load on the CPU; would have to go
back soon to manual filing, with file cabinets.

There were two orchids in a celadon Chinese bowl on the
bar, and a lady just sitting there in Laura Biogiotti sun-glas-
ses, and bright-striped Valentino boots.

THE MAN WHO
HAD NEVER BEEN
IN TACOMA

This was the fat woman on the bus, with a cast in her eye. This was before the one room-one person laws were passed.

He wore a white suit and black hat and drank whiskey in the bar. No one could tell if it was whiskey or tea, since they were shooting a film. He drank and looked around.

This was relevant. In Nicaragua, they picked the best bananas. These were shipped to USA, Canada, Australia, etc. The Nicaraguans ate the rotten or unripe bananas. Also, New Zealand sent kiwi fruits to USA, France, Germany, etc. These were used to tenderize steaks.

This diploma had a red seal, official, on it. It was signed, and stamped. It could be gotten at home. It was on a pack of matches. This was free.

After he had watered the animals, he could eat. There was cow shit on his boots. He ate looking out the window, into the air. There were no sounds, but he heard and remarked them. This was the place to be.

In the subway, a Negress beat a dapper Negro with a sweet potato. He was a diplomat, with an attaché case chained to his wrist. The woman could not contain herself.

'You high-falutin' nigger!' she yelled, flailing him. 'Damn you! You high-falutin' nigger, you!'

'Madame, please,' he said. He was going to the UN.

This was nothing. One could see trucks any time. You sat by the road, and they came. All different kinds of license plates. But he had seen all this before, anyway.

There was a Replogle globe that lit up. He had wanted it for his birthday. He had found Singapore. This was a city he dreamed of. His mother came out. She wore rubber thongs, and her legs were bare. He told her he wanted Town Host Baker's Cake and iced tea. This was his favorite. His grandfather began to talk about when he played the mellophone. This was a story he liked to tell and told. His grandfather had been in a war. At night, he would scream 'Kill them! Stop them! Kill them!'

This was just a temporary thing. This job was just for a while. This job was not a real job. This was just semi-time. It was part-time. It was not permanent. This was to get by with. It was really his second job. But actually it was really his third job, counting that week-end nights job at the service station.

Somebody practised the violin until 3 am. You could never sleep right. A drunk pounded on the floor of the apartment of the violinist.

'You fuckin' queer, Vreeland!'

Another young man with a large body came out in the hallway at odd hours sometimes. He would yell loudly.

'I'm not a fuckin' Communist! I'm not a fuckin' Communist! Goddammit, I'm not a fuckin' Communist!'

He would return then to his room.

There was a dance where they let the WAFs come. He had been in basic eight weeks and hadn't seen a woman up close. His body trembled. He did not ask any of the WAFs to dance. One WAF was pretty. She danced all the time. They said one guy — Gerringer — over in another barracks got her that night.

This was always the game they played. It was pinochle. On the train in and out of Chicago. Chicago & Northwestern Railroad. There was no other game.

On the bus you could see up their skirts. Especially in the mornings. They would sit down across from you. It had to be the right angle. This was a matter of luck. You could see all the way. Everyone did it. This was something, too.

You could see it through windows. Others. They all did it. They wanted it, too. You just had to look sharp. Keep all your lights out. They sold binoculars, didn't they? You could see it all.

The light was the thing. Half a year of light. Half a year of dark. Dark and cold. 'A cold day in Hell', he wrote on a picture he took of the base. This was his overseas tour he had requested. The first sergeant had fixed it all for him. He had smiled. It was said they gave you two things when you got there: an economy size jar of Vaseline, and a rubber glove.

The way he did was he marked it up 30 cents. At least that much. Give them lots of bone, lots of fat, fatty gristle. Maybe you could get in 10, 12 pound. It could be done. You just did it. What about the inspectors? Maybe they wouldn't come this time. What could you do?

There were other people in the bank. There were six lines of people. There were seven people in some lines. Eight, ten in others. The ceiling was high, and the floor was marble and the counters were white marble. The tellers smiled. They counted money, and smiled. There were little pillars at the sides of their windows. People coughed. It was all air-conditioned.

Bob filled the tank. They were on the highway. Later they came to Niagara Falls. The Canadian side was better, they thought. Two of them rode on the boat through the falls. At night they were in the motel. It cost $12.72 for one night in the motel. They could not find the owner in the morning. This was their first vacation in nine years. Next time, they figured on going to South Carolina.

In the apartment, it was hot and there were little lace curtains. The plastic on the chair stuck to him. The fan, though, was broken. It was a G.C. Murphy fan, Nbr 742, Avocado, and had been on special. It had overheated, and broken. He drank beer, and threw the bottles out the window, down between the walls. He liked to hear them explode when they hit. This was satisfying.

This was a big sale. The BIC pens were 3 for 39¢. They worked. Paper towels wee 2 for 39¢. Scott or Viva. Hand cream was reduced. 76¢ a jar. She had her hair fixed later. You were getting six magazines for free, they called on the telephone. *Sports Illustrated, Better Homes and Gardens, McCalls, Redbook, Argosy,* and *Time.* This was for only 49¢ a week. They said there was more.

What was that? They heard a noise, parking. He had her bra off. She let him, and looked at a large vein in his neck, full. He was sweating. This was after the football game with Parkersburg Valley. This was the big game.

There was another kid, who was fat and had long, shanky hair, oily. He did not look like a kid. They said he was eleven. He carried a cat in his arms, and a black plastic rocket gun. He sat on the porch, and looked in the street.

This Womens Lib was no good, either. It would be seen. You couldn't do that. God made man and woman, and there was marriage. After you moved to another town, things got rough, sometimes. Bake a cake, or something. This was in the late afternoon.

This college thing was the only way, too. Hadn't they told him? He didn't give a damn if they laughed, anyway. They would see; they would find out. He was worried about masturbation. He could see his hair in the sink in the mornings.

'Enter Here'. This is what the sign said.

The rings were $14.99 and $15.99. The bracelets were $7.99 and $9.99. The charms were $2.99 and $3.99. The heart lockets were $20.00, even.

They moved in when the five Chinese students moved out. They were medical students. The landlord was Polish.

'Look at how this place is,' he said.

Later he told them about young girls. He did not approve of the young girls. They came to men's apartments, and they were practically naked, the way they went around in the streets. At all hours of the night.

This war memorial had five names in the War of 1812 and there were four names in the Mexican War.

The femur is the thigh bone, and it is the largest bone in the human body. Once, in Health class, he had memorized all of the 206 bones in the human body.

All the time.

BATES COPES

Bates sits in the small kitchen shovelling in his supper, while looking at a catalog of lingerie; he utters a stream of epithets as he looks at the lissome young women attired in silky underthings of nearly all colors, many transparent. Some pull on sheer nylons while looking in a maddeningly seductive fashion at the camera. The catalog was so good you could smell it.

Who actually got to sleep with such women as these? Bates wondered. In front of whom did they wear this gear?

'I bet the photographer had a hard-on' he grunted. But maybe the photographer was a women . . . maybe they were all lesbians. Preferred each other to men, and were secretly laughing at the thought of men drooling over these photographs.

It was hot, muggy and the sweat trickled down his back even as he sat in the chair. Another stinking summer full of bugs, gnats, horseflies, bees . . . two people had been killed when a bee had gotten trapped in the cab of their pick-up truck. Birds singing so loudly they awakened you at the crack of dawn, at 5:15 or so. Pigeons cooing, doves whirring, owls whooing and a cacophony of chirping and warbling. The birds awake! Who disturbed *their* sleep? Maybe automobiles. . . . Then there were the bats, in the evening. Sitting in his living room, he'd been listening to some very fine jazz. And the black shape was suddenly circling the room in a quick, wheeling spiral — a bat. He had to knock it down with a broom, into a corner, where he'd captured it in a box, and put it in the garbage. He had not slept at all well after that for a while; every noise made him think of the bat. And the heat, this early in the summer! The heat made the old smell of the old house came out — it was a musty smell of old wood, brick dust, damp cellar, mold, drains — that he associated with Eastern houses especially. You could never air the places out properly, it seemed, and the sun was never really bright enough to dry them out fully, bleach them clean.

There was something hopeless about his life that he was beginning to recognize. Actually, he had been noticing it for about twenty years, but hoped it would go away, or change. He lacked assertiveness — the contemporary term meaning that he was not sufficiently willing to be a son-of-a-bitch, to inflict pain on others, to get what he wanted. He lacked self-confidence; lamentable. He mused on this, and stared at the remains of food on his plate; there was a little pool of congealing grease from the hamburger. He broke wind. "Jesus, I'm getting disgusting," he thought.

'Livin' like a hawg!' he then said aloud. He often spoke aloud in the apartment, and had once frightened the Jewel Tea man while in one of his monologues. But why not?

He would have to read another of these books on all the changes — the seasons, as the authors put it — in one's life . . . and also the magazine articles. In *Vogue,* which he considered a minor monthly art work and liked to read, they had articles which told you *how* to change with the times every month.

The chair on which he was sitting, mooning away, lurched to the side suddenly, and he grabbed at the table. The leg had popped out of its socket again. He should fix it, but did not know how, nor had he the motivation. Why fix these things? Some people did, though; they seemed to go through life repairing everything in their reach. They had the most amazing garages, these people, with literally everything from soup to nuts in them. And *tools* . . .they had many tools, and they almost always had *the right tool.* And if they didn't they knew which tool was the right tool, where to get it, and about how much it cost. Yet they read no books, did not know where Zimbabwe was, and often hadn't gone to college. Why did they know all this tool

stuff? What did it mean, or signify? It had to mean something. It was said they had common sense, horse sense; they
knew which end was up. They had their feet on the ground.
They knew their ass from a hole in the ground. They knew
which way the wind was blowing, and had a nest egg salted
away for a rainy day. They were never asleep at the switch,
and never got screwed by garage mechanics. Their wives
never left them, they missed no days at work and never went
crazy. They read the whole newspaper every evening.

There was a piece of paper with writing on it on the table,
and he looked absently at it. He had stuff — squibs — written down in several places, like on the backs of envelopes,
and in a small tablet, and on these slips of paper he'd empty
out of his pockets. Couldn't let an idea slip by. He now even
had a small blackboard by the sink in the kitchen. But he
suspected many people did this, were doing it. Look, for instance, at all those memo pads and such for sale now, even
in supermarkets. It was a country of enormous amounts of
secret messages scrawled on paper. Filed away, locked up,
safe deposit box, Do Not Open; all written down.

He had farted again . . . cheesy Italian pizza farts, they
were round, flat emissions that had neither the tone or vigor
of your true Anglo-Saxon flatulence. What would an Oriental fart be like? he wondered. An Arabic one — would it be
hurried, speedy, caffeinesque? There must be some neglected sub-science of flatulence, of meteoritis, of suspiratory
eructations.

Have something scheduled to do every day! The note on
the paper said. This was the considered advice of sanguine
people to him, to help him in his situation. . . . The jelly jar
in front of him, left from his hasty breakfast, was smeared
with butter, a violation he would only have committed in an
extreme hurry. But that was no excuse! he thundered at
himself. Now, when removed from the refrigerator, cold, in
the morning, it would be awful. Who would ever be able to
live with him, with such things?

Lou Reed was playing on the FM radio. He thought of

hearing Lou Reed in Iowa — probably because he was fan-
tasizing about driving his car cross-country. Probably Lou
Reed was big in Iowa. Eternity in the country. Eternity in
the city. Which was worse? Or better?

If all those secret writings, these secret diaries and jour-
nals — and now there were so many more, due to therapists,
creative writing classes, and trendy advice in mass circula-
tion magazines — *The Intensive Journal,* etc. — if all of
them were suddenly published! Actually, many of them
now were being published; that was the latest. It was more
authentic than fiction.

He looked again at the lingerie catalog. It was called
"Sheila's Secrets: Lovely Things For Modern Women".
Masturbation was a terrible drag. He looked at the women.
Who were they? They had actual names, phone numbers;
they lived somewhere, in an apartment, or house. They got
up in the morning and dressed. Did they wear this stuff to
work? Maybe they were daring like French women, wearing
erotic underthings no one knew were there, under very de-
mure exteriors; full skirts, dresses, low-heeled shoes, frilly
blouses up to the neck. That would be sexy. Was this the
secret, the hermeneutics, of lingerie? It was doubtful that
many American women would dress so, though; they were
too practical, too fearful or too liberated. He felt he might
be understanding underwear for the first time. He was getting somewhere.

But who did they go with? He kept returning to that. A
tall, handsome man; one who could make their toes curl,
legs reach for the ceiling. Despite all the rhetoric, that was it.
And if he had a big dick. Of course, this was disavowed pas-
sionately, as the rankest sexism, but his experience was
otherwise. He had seen a bumper sticker in Texas once that
read 'Happiness Is A Twelve-Incher' . He had a small dick,
fully erect, and that was definitely one of his failings. He'd
never been aware - none of the women he'd slept with had
said anything. But a man doesn't tell a woman he's sleeping
with that her breast are small, either, unless they're breaking

up, or he wants to break up.

A women in Illinois had revealed this secret to him. And it was funny, too, for she had protested that she was a virgin, or at least nearly so. Finally, in bed, he realized he was treading a path trod by many before. She had gripped his dick in her hand — she was drunk — and said, with a laugh 'But he's so short!'

He had nearly been unable to complete the act, and felt instantly shrivelled inside. As they made love, she kept asking, in a drunken slur, if she was doing it right?

'Am I doing it right? Huh? Hunnuh? Is this okay?'

There was a summer rainstorm in progress outside; a cloud-burst; just like in the movies. He had lain there in his old bed, which creaked at every move — he'd often wondered what it must've sounded like to those in the apartment below — and finally asked her what she'd meant. She then told him of her ex-boyfriend. His cock was so big she could not get her thumb and forefinger around it. In addition her arm used to get tired jerking him off, for he apparently could control his coming so well that he only came after, she said, *hours* of fucking. He would call her, and begin conversations by saying 'I had such a hard-on when I was talking to you last night' , playing with himself as they spoke. She allowed how he had really tired her, and then noted that he 'really tore a lot of girls up' . This was said with a relish and pride, that made him wince and feel even worse, and he had stared at the ceiling in the darkness.

This was it then — the bull, the stallion, the horse cock that made them swoon, giddy, when viewed, touched, taken. The phallus! All those ancient phallic processions, rites, status, cults had known the news. A short-dicked man was nowhere, a disaster, and could only turn intellectual, or get fat, eating his heart out. The big-dicked men lounged in bars grinning; some of the men he'd known in the military service would say 'She'll sing a different tune when I give her this!' It was a melancholy thought. . . .

The woman herself had had a secret. Her skin covered

her nipples totally in a transparent film, impacted them, and she was embarrassed by this and asked if he thought it was ugly. He said no, that she had beautiful breasts.

Some women had said he had a 'beautiful penis'. Fitting, esthetically, perhaps for a sculptural model, but somewhat lacking as an erotic tool. Even the maid in Shakespeare's *Antony and Cleopatra* had said that if she had the choice of where to add an inch to her husband's anatomy, it wouldn't be to his nose.

He looked down at himself. His jeans were faded; he needed a new pair. He now needed those 'full-cut' jeans, for men. He had lived much of his entire adult life in blue jeans, he thought. . . .

He had no pride in himself, that was at the core of it. He should have gone to one of the military academies, and then he would have had self-pride, and gotten a lot out of life. Or Harvard — if only he were a Harvard graduate! Would he have had 'Have something scheduled to do every day!' chalked on his little kitchen blackboard then?

The lingerie . . what woman would love him now? He was balding, had a small dick, no money, a congenitally de-viated septum, a used, badly rusting car, thick-lensed glas-ses, and was putting on weight. He took vitamins, but they turned his piss yellow, and he feared he was bringing on a kidney stone. Yet he felt he probably was suffering from all kinds of deficiencies — how could you eat nutritiously ba-lanced meals, regularly, living alone? Who even, for that matter, knew what nutritiously balanced was? Maybe he should take up eating soy beans, and jogging.

It did not look promising. No woman would ever dress like this just for him, breathless with expectation. No one would meet him like this at the airport, while other men glanced envyingly. He would instead trudge off towards the Airporter bus, his raincoat a wrinkly mess on him, and his glasses maybe even taped. Looking at himself in the mirror, he thought he was beginning to look like a technical writer.

He'd sit in bars and hope nobody would know how desperate he was, and of course they all would. How can you not look desperate, alone in a bar? He would try to keep from eating all the pretzels, or nuts, or popcorn . . . he had had conversations, though. A young person in a local bar had recently told him that 'You're stereotyped now. Your generation's stereotyped. You're getting old, man! That's why you don't understand us.'

In the morning he'd fix that jelly jar. Just throw the thing out. To have to look at a thing like that, peering into the cave of the refrigerator, which was too big anyway; he had asked his landlord several times to get him a smaller one, and also to replace the pathetic little tub he had in his bathroom, with a shower. Or at least put a shower into the tub. He had to make a note of that. And, too, that story that Joe had told him from his days living in the YMCA, about the guy who was very skinny. He had been in his room one night, and these other guys had come and pounded on his door yelling 'Open the door, or we'll beat the shit outta you!' The guy had opened the door, and they had beaten him so badly he had to be hospitalized. . . . Life at the Y, as Joe said. Had to get that down . . . there were a lot of things he felt like he was going to do some things about; he was getting it together, for sure. And he'd burn that damn lingerie catalog! Burn it.

MISS AMERICA